Room of
Dark Secrets

Michael Cole

Foremost Press
Cedarburg, Wisconsin

Also by Michael Cole

A King's Ransom
The Papyrus Document
Secrets of El Tovar Canyon
Subprime: A Novel

Published by Foremost Press
www.foremostpress.com

ISBN-10: 1-936154-52-8
ISBN-13: 978-1-936154-52-4

To my very
special friends -
Jim & Sharon Snyder

Michael

To my grandson, Elijah.
This book probably wouldn't have
been written were it not for
his interest in grimoires.

PROLOGUE

The interloper had been crouching in the snow watching the priest's every move. When the clergyman approached the fire, the intruder readied himself for action, but instead of lunging at the priest, he backed off because he did not have the book. It was only when the grey shadows of twilight were replaced by the faint glow of the fire that the priest made his move. The interloper's eyes followed the clergyman as he ignited a torch and then entered the Santa Passera Church. The interloper could hear him walk from the entrance to the pulpit where a rickety staircase led to the belfry. And although the priest trod ever so lightly on the earthen floor, the interloper, who was not far behind, could hear the shuffling of his feet. Unlike the noise of a rat, it was more pronounced, like the sound of acorns being crunched by a shoe.

The interloper followed the priest as he made his way to the belfry. The shadow the clergyman cast when he walked past the church bell was huge, the movements stealth-like.

The interloper watched the priest loosen a floorboard and remove a manuscript, the very one he had been sent to find. The priest opened the book and began reading phrases out loud. His chanting sounded rhythmic, almost melodious, like a litany during High Mass. And although the words were spoken in a tongue the interloper understood, he made little sense of them.

The interloper was a patient man. He waited until the priest, cloistered among the rats and the cobwebs, had finished reciting the ritual. When the clergyman left the belfry, the interloper followed him out of the church. The priest approached the fire, opened the book, and again started to read phrases from the ancient handwritten text.

Some called the type of book he was reading a grimoire. Most grimoires contained instructions on how to perform spells, charms and divinations, but the grimoire in his possession did much more than that. Purportedly written by King Solomon, it contained a gateway to the secret wisdom of the ancients. In addition to its pseudo-Hebraic mystical symbols, spirit conjugations and formulas for potions, elixirs and charms, the book dealt with a compendium of mystical knowledge encoded in a nonphysical plane of existence.

Manuscripts such as this were almost unheard of, particularly one that dated back to the eleventh century. They were highly valued, as they were believed to contain inherent magical powers not available in published works.

The interloper knew if the clergyman was caught reading the grimoire he could end up facing dire consequences. For the year was 1637, and the Roman Catholic Inquisition had launched an aggressive mass-suppression of peoples and views they considered heretical. Many of those accused in dealing with the occult were imprisoned and in more serious cases the Church would extract the ultimate penalty—death. Few dared to read such books openly. Some clergymen such as this priest chose to ignore the Inquisition's mandate and secretly poured over mystical texts in the hope of providing some evidence of God's existence; for surely if demons could be conjured into this earthly world, then so could angels.

The priest seemed agitated. Was it that he was unable to conjure a spirit? Or was it for some other unknown reason? The interloper did not know for certain, but he had been told by others that whoever read from this very text would come to a horrific end. The interloper wondered if the priest thought so, too, because he was about to throw the grimoire into the fire.

The interloper rushed toward the priest who attempted to stop him from grabbing the book. As the two struggled, the priest dropped the book into the burning embers, and at that very moment, the interloper shoved him into the flames. Fortunately, the book escaped serious damage. In one deft move, the interloper scooped up the grimoire and tucked it under his cloak.

Just at that moment, the interloper heard a twig snap. Or was it the crackle of the fire? He couldn't be sure, and he didn't want to stick around to find out, so he mounted his horse and sped off into the night.

CHAPTER 1

When the lights were turned off, the silence in the room became palpable. It appeared as if the amphitheater had been engulfed in a black hole, an abyss so dark that no human could penetrate.

An incandescent white light from above revealed a large intricately-carved chest the size of a steamer trunk. Positioned in the middle of the stage, it shone with such brilliance that it gave the impression it had a force of its own. An illusionist in a black tuxedo appeared. He wore a black cape and whenever he moved, one could see the cape's red lining swish from side to side. Upon removing a pair of white gloves, he waved a pointer at the chest, one similar to what an orchestra conductor would use.

Within seconds the container began to rock gently from side to side. When it stopped moving, the lid began to rise. And as it did so, several billows of crimson fumes emerged from the box. The smoke appeared innocuous at first, but once the lid disappeared from view, it became so thick that it was no longer possible to see the chest. Suddenly the smoke cleared, and in its place several demon-like creatures took form. Like a couple of Banshee jets they swished through the air, criss-crossing the stage. Faster and faster they flew until they became a blur.

The illusionist again waved his pointer. No sooner had he done so than the demon-like apparitions slowed their ascent to a snail's pace, and then imploded into puffs of black smoke.

Two thousand people gasped once they saw what next emerged from the box. At first the image was diminutive. It perched in mid-air above the box. It had the body of a dog and the face of a devil. As it became larger, its evil-looking eyes stared at the audience, and the audience stared back. Within seconds the grotesque demon-like creature filled the entire stage. Once the gargoyle became gargantuan, it let out an unworldly wail. The sound pierced through the room like a mortar shell. It was so shrill that the crystal pendants hanging from the chandeliers began to shake. Before the audience's very eyes, it contorted into a sphere. When the disc-like object exploded, dozens of flying objects circled the stage. Eventually, they reshaped themselves back into a ball, which then metamorphosed into a flying serpent. The snake-like fiend circled the amphitheater and then slowly, deliberately, reentered the chest.

For the last time that evening, the illusionist waved his pointer, and when he did, the lid reappeared. It hovered above the container and ever so slowly came to rest on top of the chest.

Frank Santino, illusionist extraordinaire, returned several times to take his bows. As usual, the audience was on its feet, the applause deafening. Finally, the curtain dropped and Frank returned to his dressing room. He was in no mood to sign autographs so he wiped the perspiration off his tanned face and changed into some casual clothes. Just as he was about to make his exit, he heard a knock on the dressing room door. If that idiot security guard let some fan get past him, he would give him a piece of his mind. When he opened the door, one of the stagehands greeted him.

"This note is for you, Mr. Santino."

The stagehand beamed when Frank handed him a twenty.

"Thank you, Mr. Santino, sir. Great show tonight."

"Glad you liked it, Pete." Frank took the envelope and closed the door. He knew it couldn't be a note from an admirer as the envelope had the unmistakable Boulevardier Hotel seal. He tore it open and upon reading the contents was overcome with a feeling of anxiety. Richard Stover, head of entertainment for the Boulevardier Hotel and Casino, wanted to talk to him. He reread the note a second time in the hope it would reveal Stover's reason for wanting to see him, but the message simply stated he should come by his office between ten and eleven the next morning. Frank crumpled the note, stashed it in his pocket, and left the amphitheater. He was quite aware that attendance at the amphitheater had been slipping lately, and he was sure this was what Stover wanted to talk to him about.

When the parking attendant brought his car around, he slipped him a ten, climbed into his new red Ferrari and headed toward the strip. Las Vegas at night was lit up like a speakeasy. Garish lights were everywhere. The gaming casinos seemed to beckon to him. Could this be his night? He lost forty thousand dollars playing craps last week. Maybe, just maybe, he could win some of that money back. He forced himself to continue driving and within minutes turned south onto a four-lane freeway. Most of the dazzle and glitter was now behind him. He would be home soon. It was only a twenty-minute drive from the casino's amphitheater to his two-story home, a drive he enjoyed because it gave him time to unwind and reflect on the day.

Frank never knew his father. He wasn't even sure if his mother knew who he was. But he had many "uncles." One in particular taught him how to do magic tricks. He never forgot the look of amazement in his mother's eyes when he made a coin disappear. In retrospect, that was probably a defining moment in his life. Frank was hooked. He liked nothing better than to perform in front of a crowd, and so he became an entertainer.

Unlike most magicians, he had been lucky. He was only twenty when he landed a job assisting a master conjuror who performed in a casino on the Nevada side of Lake Tahoe. Over the years, the older man had taught him all of his illusionary extravaganzas, particularly the ones that dealt with an occult theme. People loved to see demon-like apparitions. Maybe it was because they wanted to believe that the spirit world actually existed.

Frank worked for him till the illusionist retired. Because he had been taught the secret of how to create all of his holographic images, he took over the act, and in some cases even improved upon it.

Four and a half years ago, almost to the day, an opportunity of a lifetime had presented itself. The corporation that owned the casino in Tahoe was opening the Boulevardier, a five-thousand-room hotel casino with the largest amphitheater in Las Vegas. Richard Stover, the director of entertainment, wanted a show that dealt with the occult and offered Frank a headliner's job.

This was a dream come true. He had accepted the lucrative offer and had signed a five-year contract. The casino had only one major stipulation; that he produce different illusions each year. He was paid seven thousand dollars a performance. That was a princely sum considering he put on one show a day, six days a week, forty-two weeks out of the year. The other ten weeks, for which he was not paid, he used to develop new holographic acts for the ensuing year.

When he thought of the crumpled note in his pocket, he again wondered why Stover wanted to see him. Maybe it had nothing to do with the show's attendance. Maybe it was about the gambling tab he had run up at the casino. He downshifted into second, and when he pressed down on the accelerator, the car took off like a rocket. He was already paying a fortune for car insurance so he figured another speeding ticket wouldn't matter.

Frank wasn't about to let a note from Stover ruin his evening. "After all," he muttered, "tonight is tonight, and I'll deal with to-morrow when it comes."

CHAPTER 2

Five more minutes and Frank would be home and in the arms of the woman he had recently married. He had been a headliner for four years when Dottie entered his life. She was a Vegas showgirl who used to perform in a chorus line at a hotel nearby. She came to see his show one day, and after the performance asked for an autograph. He was instantly smitten. Maybe it was because she had full, pouting lips or a pair of legs long enough to stretch all the way to Los Angeles. She had given him a look that said, "I'm here, I'm available, and if you want me, you can have me."

He still recalled the attention she received when he took her to dinner. He loved the way people stared at her whenever she entered a room. No matter where they went, sooner or later all eyes would be on her. She exuded a sexual magnetism that made men covet her openly. Women would stare at her, too. Whether it was in envy or resentment, he did not know. He had decided to marry her so no other man would ever get the chance of fulfilling his fantasy.

Dottie was a looker; there was no mistake about that. She had straight blonde hair cropped in that shaggy look so popular among Vegas showgirls. She also had an hourglass figure that curved in all the right places and a smile that could melt Antarctica. Her most outstanding feature was her legs. They were dancer legs; long, tanned, athletic and tapered. When she wore her four-inch stiletto heels, she was an inch or so taller than he, but that didn't bother him.

Gorgeous women in Vegas weren't exactly in short supply, particularly to a headliner. Before Dottie, he had routinely dated exotic-looking showgirls, but most reminded him of mannequins, beautiful to look at and nice to fondle, but empty on the inside. Dottie was different. Dottie had charisma. Dottie could also carry on a halfway intelligent conversation after sex. But above all, she had the uncanny ability to make people feel good about themselves.

He thought it ironic that he had ended up marrying a showgirl. His mother had been one. He had worshipped her. Even though she had been dead for many years, he still remembered her caring ways. It hadn't been easy for her to raise him; he knew that. As a single mother, money had been tight, but somehow she managed.

Just as Frank pulled into his driveway, a woman dressed in a skimpy bikini climbed into her car. By the looks of her, she was spaced out, probably on coke. Much to his chagrin, Dottie had again extended an open invitation to the freeloaders she called friends to swim in their pool. He had begged her to cut her ties with the hangers-on, and she had promised she would, but then again Dottie seldom kept her promises. He knew most of the people she invited were either broke or soon would be. "Damn her," Frank mumbled. "I told her I wanted to come home to some peace and quiet. All she ever wants to do is party, party, party."

He parked his car, entered the house, and headed for the pool. He wished his mother could see it. That and the sprawling house he and Dottie lived in. It was a far cry from the one-room apartment he had lived in as a kid. The two of them certainly didn't need five bedrooms, but Dottie had fallen in love with the house. Upon Dottie's insistence, he had spent a hundred thousand dollars updating the home. Frank thought it looked just fine, but Dottie wanted to have that "Tuscan" look. The living and dining rooms had coffered ceilings, and the sprawling kitchen had more stone and granite than a rock quarry.

The music was so loud Frank was sure he'd get another complaint from one of the neighbors. A few men and women were in the pool. Some people were reclining on lounge chairs either drunk, high on weed, or both. But most of Dottie's friends were hovering around their hostess, absorbed in what she had to say.

When Dottie spotted Frank, she waved for him to come join her. As always, she was the best-looking woman there, a queen bee overseeing her entourage. She had on one of those string bikinis that left nothing to the imagination. When he didn't make a move towards her, she sauntered toward him in those high heels with a glass of champagne in each hand.

Frank had been annoyed that she had invited all those people, but he became downright angry when he spotted a number of empty bottles of Dom Perignon. Christ, he thought. Doesn't she realize they cost a hundred twenty bucks a bottle? He had been married to Dottie just long enough to know that now was not the time to make a scene. He'd wait till the party was over, and then he would talk to her about the money she was spending. Did she think he had a goose that laid golden eggs? At times like this, Frank thought that maybe marrying Dottie had been a mistake.

She was only inches from his face when she cooed, "Did my honey have a tough day?"

He took one of the glasses she offered and drained the drink. He drank the other glass, too. As always, the wine calmed his nerves.

Dottie rubbed one of her knees gently against his crotch. "Why is it I find you so irresistible?"

He backed off a little in case people were watching. "I don't know why," came the throaty reply.

She placed a hand against his face and caressed his cheek. "It's because you turn me on. God, would you believe I'm wet already?"

Frank's anger disappeared much like his apparitions. He no longer cared about the spent bottles of champagne, and he certainly didn't give a damn about the summons he had received from Richard Stover. At forty-eight years of age, Frank Santino was as hard as a rock. Although he wanted to take her that very moment, he decided to prolong the anticipation for he knew it would only be a matter of time before she sent him into a land of ecstasy, a land where there was no Richard Stover.

CHAPTER 3

Frank felt as if his head was a bird's nest and the hawk in his brain was about to take flight. He groaned when he recalled what had happened the previous evening. He had drunk too much champagne, which certainly was not unusual when he was around Dottie. He felt around for her, but she was not in bed. When he glanced at the clock, he sprang bolt upright. It was half past nine, and he was supposed to be in Stover's office between ten and eleven.

Frank took a quick shower, shaved, stepped into a pair of pants, and threw on a shirt. He figured he didn't have time for breakfast; besides, Dottie wasn't around to fix it. She was most likely out spending his money. Between her manicurist, hair stylist, personal trainer, tennis coach and shrink, she was costing him a bundle. And then there were her clothes. She had a closet full of designer dresses that cost a small fortune. Not to mention the footwear. He still couldn't fathom why a woman had to have five dozen pairs of shoes.

Frank decided he had to put her on a budget. Either that or declare bankruptcy. He laughed at the thought. His net monthly income from the show came to well over a hundred thousand dollars. A lot of money, even for a headliner, but it all seemed to find its way into other people's pockets instead of his.

Frank knew he had to stop gambling. He never thought he'd become addicted to a crap table. In the beginning when he'd place small bets he would usually win. Then when he began to put out some serious cash, the house almost always took all of his chips. His problem was he didn't know when to quit. On the few occasions when he was ahead, he'd keep trying to win more, and sooner or later his stack of chips, no matter how large, would dwindle away.

By the time he climbed into the Ferrari, it was ten fifteen. He'd make a quick stop at Starbucks and barring heavy traffic, he figured he'd reach the casino well before eleven. Frank glanced in the rearview mirror. The telltale signs of age hadn't caught up with him yet. His chin was still firm and there were no wrinkles beneath his eyes. When he was a youngster, he fell out of a tree and broke his nose. The bone had never been set properly. It bothered him so much that he had gone to a plastic surgeon who reshaped it into a work of art.

Frank was not naïve enough to think that Dottie had come on to him because of his looks. Some said he had an interesting face with his ruddy complexion, long sideburns, and neatly cropped, Van Dyke beard, but handsome he was not. He had a shock full of black, curly hair and a brooding look about him, which Dottie claimed she liked.

What set Frank apart from many men was he could wear clothes. He was trim because he kept in shape and whether it was a pair of Levis or a three-thousand-dollar suit, he would always stand out in a crowd. He'd be fifty soon, but he looked much younger, probably because he had no signs of grey hair, not even around the temples.

It didn't bother him that he was twenty years older than Dottie. He didn't think the age difference was a concern to her either, at least not as long as he could afford to provide her with a lifestyle she had grown accustomed to.

The parking attendant recognized him instantly. "Good morning, Mr. Santino," he said cheerfully. "I hear that White Lightning is running on the grass at Santa Anita today. It might pay off to place a 'C' note on him to win."

Frank handed him a hundred-dollar bill. "Do it for me, Charlie. If the nag wins, you can keep half the money, but I want my hundred back."

The attendant's eyes lit up. "Thank you, Mr. Santino, sir! I'll park your car out in front if you like."

Frank gave Charlie a wink. "I don't care where you park it as long as you don't spin any broadies. The last time you got behind the wheel of my car, I barely had enough tread on the tires to make it back home."

Charlie laughed. "I promise I'll be careful."

Frank walked into the lobby of the Boulevardier Hotel and Casino as if he owned the place. All the help knew he was a headliner and a good tipper as well. When he walked past one of the crap tables, he glanced at his watch. He still had a few minutes, so he handed a fistful of hundred-dollar bills to the croupier, and in exchange received ten black chips. He placed them all on the pass line, said a silent prayer, and threw the dice. The cubes hit the felt-lined table, rolled end over end a couple of times, and much to his delight a four and a three came up.

"Winner here!" the croupier yelled, trying to draw attention to the table. Frank left the chips undisturbed, and threw the dice again. This time an eleven came up. Without being asked, the croupier upgraded Frank's chips. That was the standard practice. The larger the chip's denomination, the more money people would bet. Instead of twenty black chips, Frank was given four five-hundred-dollar chips. He placed all of them on the pass line. A crowd was beginning to form around the table. Like vultures, they hovered behind Frank trying to determine whether they should take the proverbial plunge.

"Come on in," Frank said. "The water is fine." He rolled the dice and much to his surprise a six came up. Frank glanced at the person standing to his right. "Wouldn't you know it? Just when I have to leave, I roll my lucky number."

Frank pressed the six by placing another four thousand dollars worth of chips behind the pass line. He blew on the dice and with the flick of the wrist threw the cubes onto the table's back-splash. It took three tries, but he managed to roll his number.

"Winner here!" the croupier yelled.

More people were trying to edge their way to the table and many who had been watching were placing chips on the pass line hoping that the dice the well-dressed man was holding would continue to favor them.

Frank glanced at his watch. Shit, he was already twenty minutes late for his meeting with Stover. His first inclination had been to cash in his chips. The last thing he wanted was to upset Stover. "Screw Stover," he mumbled. He was in the middle of a hot streak, and he sure as hell wasn't going to walk away from the table. Not now.

CHAPTER 4

Frank had only been at the crap table for thirty minutes, and it looked as if every person in the casino had gathered to watch the "big winner." He was placing so many bets at one time that an additional croupier came over so he could help keep an eye on all of the action.

Anyone who plays craps knows that sooner or later the inevitable happens. Frank had to roll a four, which was his number, and a seven popped up. The players who had been betting on Frank to win groaned, while those who had been placing bets on the don't pass line collected their winnings.

Within a short period of time, Frank had accumulated fourteen thousand dollars. He pushed the stack of chips in front of the pit boss. "I'm in a rush, Charlie. Would you mind applying these toward my marker?"

"Will do, Mister Santino."

The pit boss counted the chips, wrote a figure on a piece of paper, and after signing the note, handed it to Frank. "Come back soon, Mr. Santino."

"Thanks, buddy. I'm outa here." And with that parting comment, he headed for Stover's office, which was on the second floor. There were so many people milling around the elevators that Frank decided to take the stairs. He was sweating by the time he arrived. Booze did that to him, particularly champagne. He was sure that the couple lines of coke he had snorted hadn't helped either. He faced Stover's secretary, a blonde with a plastic smile. "I have an appointment with Mr. Stover."

"Go right in, Mr. Santino. He's been expecting you."

The door to Stover's office was closed. Frank hesitated, but only for a moment. The secretary did say to go in. He decided the proper thing to do would be to knock first.

Behind the desk, the size of a ping-pong table, sat a dark driven man. If he hadn't been draped in an expensive Italian suit, his bulk would have projected the image of a hungry bear foraging for meat. Stover had charcoal black hair slicked down with some grease, most likely pomade. It appeared as if someone had landed a meat cleaver on his chin, the cleft of distinction as some would say.

Frank always wondered if Stover had been a hood. He certainly looked like one, either that or a stevedore. Frank didn't much care to associate with people who had no taste. To say Stover was garish would be an understatement. Frank thought Stover had to be col-orblind for he always leaned toward monochromatic colors; black suit, black linen shirt, black tie. He would have given five to one odds that his underwear was also black. Who in hell did he think he was, an undertaker?

Stover could be jovial, even charming at times, but Frank had seen his dark side once, and it hadn't been a pretty sight. The last thing he wanted was to cross swords with a guy whose fuse was shorter than a cigarette butt. Stover was one of the most powerful men in the entertainment business. Frank had to admit the man had a lot of clout. He could make you or break you with a phone call. Frank just wanted to know what the S.O.B. had in mind so he could get back to the crap table. Winning streaks didn't come by all that often, and he felt this was going to be his lucky day.

When Stover saw Frank, he stood to greet him. In order to shake Stover's hand, Frank had to wade through an expanse of car-pet about as deep as the sand in the Sahara Desert. When he finally was close enough, Stover extended one of his meaty paws for Frank to shake. He had a bone-crunching grip, the kind that makes you wonder if you're ever going to be able to use your hand again.

Frank immediately noticed Stover's trinkets. How could any-one miss them? The man must have had at least a pound of gold on each wrist. Expensive, but garish, Frank thought. He wondered if Stover knew the meaning of understated elegance. Although his clothes were expensive, Frank decided that Richard Stover was the antithesis of Armani, definitely a dresser with no taste.

"You are late," Stover admonished him in a raspy voice, the kind that gives off mental odors of tobacco and alcohol. "What happened? Did you run into a crap table?"

Frank wasn't about to let Stover intimidate him. "As a matter of fact, I did. How could I help it? You guys shouldn't place them so close to the elevators, you know."

Stover laughed. "Knowing you, if there was one in the middle of an uncharted island, you'd find it."

As usual, Stover had a comeback. He always did. Frank sat. He felt uneasy around this man. Maybe it was because of his eyes. They bore into you like a drill. Stover leaned back in his chair, took out a cigar, and popped it in his mouth. He chewed on it for a few seconds and then took it out.

"Listen, I know you must get ready for tonight so I'll come right to the point. I don't know if you noticed, but ticket sales for the show have dropped off. You aren't packing 'em in like you used to."

"The economy is in the toilet," Frank countered, then added, "All of Vegas is hurting right now."

"Yeah, I know. Gambling is off by twenty-seven percent. That number would most likely be higher if you stopped playing craps." Stover tilted his head back and roared. That was Stover, always enjoying a joke at someone else's expense.

It was a humiliating statement, but Frank said nothing. Stover's comment made him wonder if everyone in Vegas was aware of his gambling problem.

Stover turned serious. "When does your contract run out?"

Frank wondered if Stover's hatchet was about to fall. Why else would the S.O.B. be asking such a question? He knew damn well when his contract was up. "Three and a half months, give or take a week," he replied, trying to keep his voice steady.

Stover twirled the cigar in his tobacco-stained fingers. Then he put it in his mouth and chewed on it for a while. When he removed it, one end of the cigar was wet and frayed.

"I'm not allowed to light the damn thing," Stover said. "Corporate put the kibosh on smoking so I just chew on it. It helps me think." He narrowed his steely eyes to mere slits. The eyes of a predator in search of some hidden opportunity, Frank thought.

"I don't want you to get the wrong idea. You are a great performer, have been for years, but your act . . . well, it needs some sprucing up. Our show is one of the few on the strip that isn't sold out."

Frank felt the knot in his stomach tighten. "What do you mean by sprucing up?"

Stover again chewed on the cigar and then threw it into a brass cuspidor. "Did you know there's a magician in France who can actually move objects with his mind?"

"You mean telekinesis?"

Stover's smile was broad. Nonetheless, it looked mendacious. "I don't know what the hell you call it. All I know is he can make things like beach balls, hats and hoops fly around a room."

"I'm sure it's just a trick. It has to be," Frank said.

"I don't know if it's a trick nor do I care, but I can tell you this. That Frenchman has received rave reviews. I sent one of my men to Paris to check him out. He told me the guy can also levitate. I mean he can actually raise himself off the floor by a couple of feet. My man placed his hands above him, beneath him and every which way, and there weren't any wires."

The knot in Frank's stomach was so tight now he had trouble catching his breath. "You actually flew someone to Paris, France, to check him out?"

Stover's forehead became etched with deep furrows. There was also a gleam in his eyes. "Of course I did. Do you actually think I'd consider hiring someone who wasn't legit?"

It would have been less painful if Stover had stabbed him with a pitchfork. "Are you saying you aren't going to renew my contract?"

"I'm hoping it won't come to that. As I said before, you put on a good show, but your apparitions are yesterday's news. People lose interest quickly in an act these days. They want to see something unique, something spectacular, something no one else can do. They want to go back to Des Moines, Missoula, or wherever the hell they came from and tell their hick friends that they saw the performance of their lives. Know what I mean? We want those hicks to come see our show."

Frank decided it would be best not to respond to a question like that. What did he think? That he could walk on water?

Stover took out a fresh cigar and with a cutter the size of a guillotine snipped off the end. "I asked you a question. Can you or can't you come up with a new show?"

Frank swallowed hard. Beads of sweat began to appear on his forehead. "You mean one without any holographic images?"

"Now you've got it!" Stover said, all smiles. "People are getting tired of seeing devils and demons. Reality, that's what they want. Not smoke and mirror stuff." Stover lifted his large frame out of the chair, a sure sign the meeting was over. He patted Frank on the back. "Let me know how you make out. Call me when you are ready to put on a demonstration, and I'll get the brass together. They'll be the ones who'll decide whether you stay or go. All things being equal, we'd rather have you as a headliner than some Frenchman who probably doesn't even speak English."

Frank was almost to the door, when Stover added, "You have sixty days tops. If you can't come up with something by then, we'll have to replace you."

Frank barely managed to reach the restroom before throwing up. After splashing some water on his face, he bypassed the crap tables and headed straight for the parking lot. It would have been easier if a doctor had told him he only had sixty days to live. He didn't think any magician had actually mastered levitation, including the Frenchman Stover had mentioned. Did Stover expect him to defy gravity? Hell, no one on earth could do that. Whatever that magician did had to be a trick. However, as Stover had said, it didn't really make much difference. He had driven home his point. If Frank didn't come up with a completely new show in two months' time, he would be finished.

Once in his car, Frank concentrated on the road. He shifted the Ferrari from first to second, and when the tachometer needle was approaching the redline, he placed the gearshift lever into third and popped the clutch. The car literally flew off the pavement. Frank had promised himself he would drive within the speed limit, but he had to get home, he had to think. If he lost his job, what would he do? Sure, he could get another, but he doubted if it would be as a headliner, and certainly not at his current salary. He wasn't about to become a warm-up act for some topless review. Hell, it had been so long since he'd popped eggs out of people's ears that he had forgotten how.

Frank sighed. Deception. That was what magic was all about. You get people to look at one hand while you do something with the other. Well, it wasn't quite as simple as that. He broke out in a cold sweat. News traveled fast in Vegas. One minute you were in the groove, and the next minute you were in a landfill with trash for a blanket.

Frank formed an image of himself working at some traveling carney show, hawking tickets for his own act like a common street vendor.

But it was only when he veered off the freeway that the ramifications of losing his job really sunk in. Dottie would leave him. He was certain of that. As much as she said she loved him, she'd find some well-heeled guy who would be able to afford her extravagant lifestyle. And then there was all this money he owed. How the hell was he supposed to pay his gambling debts without a job? He had markers all over town. The men who ran the casinos where he owed money would only be patient for so long. Then, if he didn't pay up, they'd send some goon to break his arm or maybe a leg.

The problem was that Frank knew very little about magic, real 'magick.' His strength lay in his ability to create holographic images that looked so real some people watching his show were convinced he could actually conjure spirits. He became angry. Sure, they paid him well, but he worked six days a week. What the hell did Stover want? Blood?

Once he calmed down a little, Frank started to think things through. Although Stover had given him an impossible assignment, at least he had been fair. He could have hired the French magician, but instead he was giving him a chance. Frank vowed he would do his damnedest to come up with an entirely new show, an act so spectacular that Stover and the people he worked for would offer him another contract. At the moment he didn't have the vaguest idea what it would be, but he knew feeling sorry for himself wasn't going to provide a solution.

Frank decided the best thing to do was take a nap. If he didn't, he might screw up his performance. After the show, he'd go home and think.

There had to be an answer. There just had to be, and he was determined to find one.

CHAPTER 5

By the time Frank had completed his performance, he felt as if someone had strapped a two-hundred-pound weight to his shoulders. Not only was he tired and depressed, but he was also scared. He knew it would take a miracle for him to come up with an act that would guarantee him his job. The problem was he was an ordinary man who was asked to perform an extraordinary feat.

When he arrived at the house, Dottie was lounging by the pool with her usual companions. He gave her a kiss. "I'm going to turn in early, hon."

"Come on, Frankie. I've been waiting for you to come home. It's only a little after twelve. Share a few lines with us."

"Not tonight. I have to fly to L.A. in the morning, and I plan on catching an early flight."

"Can I come with you? I just love Rodeo Drive."

That's just what Frank did not need. Rodeo Drive contained a string of some of the most expensive boutiques in the world. "Maybe some other time. I'm going there strictly on business."

When Frank was alone in his bedroom, he went online. Antiquarian bookstores weren't exactly on every street corner, but he did manage to find three in the Los Angeles area. He booked an eight o'clock flight to L.A., put some reading material in a briefcase, and turned in for the night. The idea had come to him quite spontaneously. If he were to find any information on levitation or telekinesis, it would be in a shop that dealt with rare out-of-print books. He knew one of the best-known magicians who had ever lived was Cornelius Agrippa who in 1533 published a book that dealt with mysticism. Maybe, just maybe, he'd get lucky and find it or one like it.

It was nine-thirty when Frank pulled out of the airport parking lot in the rental car. Much to his disappointment, the shop nearest the airport was closed. When he entered the second store, he was greeted by an affable man who appeared to be in his late eighties. "Looking for something in particular?" the old man asked.

"Yes. I was wondering if by chance you had a copy of Cornelius Agrippa's book."

The bookseller nodded his head in understanding. "You must be referring to *Libri Tres de Occulta Philosophia*."

"All I know is he was a famous magician. I don't know the title of his book."

"Three books."

"I beg your pardon," Frank said.

"Agrippa wrote three books. I have two of them. Which one would you like to see?"

"I really don't know."

Frank decided that although the man in front of him was quite old, there was absolutely nothing wrong with his mind.

The bookseller took on the droll pose of a grumpy initiate. "Well, if you tell me what you are after, maybe I can help."

"I was looking for a book that might provide some clues on levitation. Either that or telekinesis."

The shop owner's eyebrows arched. "You don't want much, do you?" He gave the matter some thought. "I only know of one grimoire that might contain such information."

"I'm sorry, a what?"

"A grimoire. Books on mysticism and the occult are called grimoires."

"Okay. So do you have this grimoire?"

"Not anymore."

Frank's optimism waned. "You mean there is nothing else on the market I can buy that would help me?"

"Oh, there are hundreds of books on mysticism, maybe more, but if you are asking me if any of them would teach you how to move objects with your mind, the answer is no."

"I appreciate your honesty," Frank said. "At least you saved me a lot of time. I probably would have ended up buying books that would have been of no use to me."

"You would only need to get ahold of one. It's a handwritten manuscript attributed to the teachings of the Israelite King Solomon. The original grimoire was most likely written in Babylonia in the eighth century some three hundred years after Solomon's death. It was known as the *Magical Treatise of Solomon*. Two hundred years later, the book was translated into Italian. Actually, I believe two copies were made. They were penned by hand as the printing press hadn't been invented yet. Handwritten books on 'magick' and the occult are supposed to have a greater import than printed copies. That's probably hogwash, but people during that period in history really believed they were quite effective in conjuring demons . . . or holding them at bay."

The old man sucked in some air and let it out. "For your information, the grimoires I just mentioned were renamed *The Testament of Solomon*. They supposedly reveal information as to how a person can train his mind to move objects from one place to another."

Frank was now convinced the shopkeeper had a thousand megahertz mind. "How come do you know so much about these . . . what do you call them?"

"Grimoires. I sold *The Testament of Solomon* fairly recently. Actually, I was responsible for bringing the buyer and seller together. I had a chance to take a quick look at it. The book is utterly amazing. Not only does it contain insights into high magick, but it also allows a reader to attain a state of mind that enables him to gain access to the akashic records."

"Sorry," Frank said. "I'm not really into mysticism. What are the akashic records?"

Just as Frank had asked the question, the telltale jingle of a bell caught the bookseller's attention. Someone had just opened the door to the shop. "Excuse me, will you?" he said. "It's a customer who has come by to pick up a book."

Frank patiently waited for the idle chitchat to end. Finally, after some cash had exchanged hands, the customer left.

"Where were we?" asked the shopkeeper. "Ah, yes, the akashic records. Akasha is a Sanskrit word that means 'sky' or 'space.' Akashic records are actually a compendium of knowledge. To put it in laymen's terms, it's a 'universal computer' that contains all knowledge of human experience. Some refer to it as the 'Mind of God.' "

This was very interesting, but what Frank needed to know was how he could purchase the book. "Could you locate a copy?"

"The person who bought one of the copies is a wealthy industrialist. Lives right here in Los Angeles as a matter of fact. His name is Jonathan Hollingsworth. If you asked him, he might let you take a peek at it. But knowing him, he would never let it out of his sight. Collectors are a strange breed. I should know. I've been dealing with the likes of Hollingsworth for over fifty years. When I sold him the book, he told me he would never part with it. The man has one of the largest privately-owned grimoire collections in the world. This particular book is his pride and joy."

"You said there were two books. Where is the other one?"

"It's in the Vatican Library."

"How do you know the Vatican has a copy?"

"It was quite a coincidence, but shortly after I sold the grimoire, I acquired a rather unusual piece of correspondence. I say this because of the papal seal that's affixed to it. I came across it quite by accident at an estate sale in Paris." The bookseller shuffled over to a nearby shelf and extracted a leather binder. Inside the folder in a plastic sheath was a document. At least that's what Frank thought it was. It looked old and withered, just like the man holding it, but the hanging papal seal, as well as the gold thread that was attached to it, was well preserved. The seal itself was about the size of a twenty-dollar gold piece.

Frank picked up a magnifying glass lying nearby and examined the article. The cursive writing on the parchment was somewhat faded. He attempted to read it, but it was written in a language he couldn't understand. The seal was made of wax and on its face was a rendition of a pope. Below his picture was the name, Alexander the VII.

"Were you able to read the writing?" Frank asked.

"It's a letter of gratitude." The bookseller picked up a magnifying glass and pored over the text for what seemed an eternity. Finally, he said. "Sorry it took so long, but it's in Latin and I wanted to make sure I'd be accurate in the translation. The letter is addressed to an archbishop. His name is Alberto Dominique. Here's what it says: 'On behalf of His Eminence, I thank you for recovering *The Testament of Solomon*. Historical works such as this grimoire are extremely important as it is from books like these that we learn about our Christian heritage.' The letter is signed by Cardinal Marcelo Cervini."

The bookseller continued to scrutinize the text. "There is also a date. It's somewhat faded and hard to read, but I believe I can make out the month and the year. May of 1637."

Frank's curiosity was piqued. He figured the grimoire the bookseller had described earlier had to be special. It was now obvious to Frank why this fellow Jonathan Hollingsworth wouldn't part with his copy. It was also apparent the Vatican thought their copy was important. Frank pointed to the ancient parchment. "Is this for sale?"

"Everything in this shop is for sale. Do you want to buy it?"

"Call it intuition, but something tells me it might come in handy."

After some protracted negotiation, Frank handed the shopkeeper six one-hundred-dollar bills. He also wrote his name and telephone number on the back of one of his cards. "If you and your wife are ever in Vegas, call me and let me know. I'd be happy to provide you with a couple of tickets to my show." As an afterthought, he added. "If you happen to think of another book that might fill my needs, please let me know."

Frank didn't bother to drive to the other bookstore. Instead, he returned the rental car and caught an earlier flight back to Vegas. It was early afternoon when he arrived and as usual, Dottie wasn't home. It was just as well because he was in a foul mood. He headed for the amphitheater.

Once in his dressing room, he fixed himself a drink. God, he wished he had a couple of lines of coke to calm his nerves. He was about to pour himself a second shooter when an idea popped into his head. For the life of him, he didn't know why he hadn't thought of it before.

CHAPTER 6

Frank wasn't overly religious, but being that he and Dottie were brought up as Catholics, both usually went to church most Sundays, probably more out of habit than for any other reason. As a matter of practice, Frank also made generous monthly contributions to Saint Mary's in Las Vegas, which was the church he and Dottie normally attended. The very next day, he made an appointment to see Father Donovan.

When Frank arrived at Saint Mary's, he was ushered into the priest's office. Donovan stood to greet him. "Hello, Frank. What can I do for you?"

"What can you tell me about the Vatican Library?"

"I've heard it has a fabulous collection of books, some of them quite old. I've been to the Vatican, but I've never been inside the library."

"There is a book there I need to see. Do you think you could arrange it?"

The priest laughed. "You're joking, aren't you?"

"No. I'm dead serious."

Father Donovan pointed to a nearby chair. "I think you'd better have a seat." Donovan sank into the chair behind a desk that had definitely seen better days. He talked mainly with his hands, trailing highways of smoke with his fingers into the air. "Until recently, the Vatican Library had been closed to all but a privileged few. Only clerics who inhabited the papal palace and its environs were allowed inside. Now, on a limited basis, the Vatican allows outsiders to conduct research there. You know, university professors, scholars and the like."

"I'm a magician," Frank said. "Does that mean they won't let me in?"

Donovan shrugged. "I don't know. Is this really important?"

"You could say it is. My job hinges on it."

Donovan's expression was a quizzical mask. He rummaged inside his desk and found a card. "I can't really help you, but maybe this lady can. She is a regular churchgoer here, just like you."

Frank glanced at the card. "What in hell . . . sorry, I mean what in the heck does a biblical archeologist do?"

Donovan chuckled. "It's okay, Frank. I've heard the word before. Now to answer your question. A biblical archeologist makes a study of the bible, but not in quite the same way that you or I might. Give the lady a call. In fact, I'll call her myself and tell her you will be contacting her."

Frank rose and shook the priest's hand. "Thank you, Father. I really appreciate this."

"You're welcome. Will I see you this Sunday?"

"You can count on it. Dottie and I are planning to attend the eleven o'clock Mass."

Once Frank was outside, he took a closer look at the card the priest had given him. On it was the name Denise Hansen. Below the name were the words, "Biblical Archeologist, Clark Foundation." There was also a phone number.

The next morning Frank arrived in front of a large multi-story building. Upon entering the foyer, he spotted a directory. The Clark Foundation was on the eighth floor. He didn't have a clue what the foundation did nor did he care. When he entered the suite, a pert young receptionist led him to a closed door. She knocked twice, opened it, and said, "Your nine o'clock appointment is here."

The woman behind the desk stood to greet him. She looked as grim as a schoolmarm, all business. "You must be Mr. Santino." She waved at a chair alongside a small conference table. "Please, won't you have a seat?"

Frank cleared his throat. "Before I tell you why I'm here, would you mind telling me what you do? I mean, it's not that I'm trying to be nosey, but just exactly what is a biblical archeologist?"

When Denise Hansen smiled, she looked as if a piece of toffee was stuck to her teeth. "Believe me, Mr. Santino, you are not the first person to ask. Most people believe our job is to prove that the Bible is historically correct, when in reality nothing could be further from the truth. What we do is raise more questions about the Hebrew Bible as well as the New Testament than we provide answers."

"Doesn't that put you at odds with Father Donovan?"

"No. Not really. I don't question the existence of God, Jesus Christ, or the Virgin Mary, Mr. Santino. You see, biblical archeology as it is practiced today challenges as well as confirms the stories of the Bible. Some things described in the Bible really did happen while others did not. The biblical narratives about Abraham, Moses and Solomon probably reflect some historical memories of people and places, but the 'larger than life' portraits of the Bible are unrealistic and are contradicted by archeological evidence. Now that I've explained what I do, what is it that I can help you with?"

"Well, funny you should mention Solomon," Frank said. "Because in a way that's why I'm here. Can you tell me about the Vatican Library?"

"I've done research there. Why do you ask?"

Frank told her about the antiquarian bookseller and Solomon's grimoire. He also told her there was a copy in the Vatican Library. "What would I have to do in order to see the book?"

Her gaze turned crystalline, distant. "You really are serious, aren't you?"

"Of course I am. Do you think I'm the kind of person who would waste your time?"

"No. Of course not. I'll answer your question as best as I can. One would have to make a written request on a standardized form the Vatican uses. The questions you'll be asked are very specific. Not only would you have to state your occupation, but you would also have to indicate the type of research you are doing. Unfortunately, even if the grimoire were to exist, my read on it is this. A magician who wants to gather information on levitation would be denied access to the book. The priest who would be reviewing your application would most likely feel that your request is not only self serving, but frivolous as well."

Frank had gathered as much, but he wasn't the type of person who gave up easily. "Okay, let's say the book contains information about the wisdom of the ancients and someone like you were to . . ."

She began to spit in syllables. "You can stop right there, Mr. Santino. I'm not about to compromise my professional standing with the Vatican if that's what you were about to ask me to do."

"Sorry, I didn't mean to offend you."

Her face softened a little. "No offense taken. I must say the cardinal or monsignor who ultimately reviews such applications might find the topic intriguing." Denise Hansen stood and offered her hand. "Sorry I can't be the one to help you."

Frank left Hansen's office in despair. A biblical archeologist would have been the perfect proxy. Not only did Hansen have the necessary credentials, but she had done research at the Vatican.

No sooner had Frank opened the door to his car, than his cell phone chimed. "Hi, it's Dottie."

"What's up?"

"I wanted to let you know Max is going to spend a few days with us. He's driving in from San Francisco."

Frank sighed. "He probably wants another loan. I like your brother, I really do, but if I'm not mistaken he's been going to college for seven years now."

"Maybe so, but he's not a professional student," Dottie said defensively. "But I must admit he has been somewhat indecisive." Her voice perked up. "He told me today he finally knows what he wants out of life."

Frank had heard all this before. "And what's that?"

"To be a college professor," Dottie said proudly. "He's thinking of going for a doctorate in philosophy."

Frank thought that was a useless major, unless, of course, one was to teach the subject. "Okay. I'll loan your brother some money so he can continue to stay in school. Hell, I should just give it to him because he'll never pay me back."

"Don't you dare!" Dottie said. "Max has a lot of pride. He won't take the money unless it's a loan."

Or unless he's earned it, Frank thought, for at that moment another idea came to mind.

CHAPTER 7

Instead of his customary afternoon nap, Frank took his laptop and rushed to the amphitheater. Once inside his dressing room, he went online and tried to acquire a rudimentary understanding of the akashic records, which he quickly discovered was an extremely difficult concept to grasp. It was like shadowboxing with illusions.

The very idea that the ancients had access to a library that contained all knowledge of human experience seemed too far-fetched. He was also surprised that many brilliant minds of the day believed such records existed. Even Isaac Newton, who for some inexplicable reason seemed to prefer the classical geometry of ancient Greece to the analytical algorithms of calculus he had invented. The more Frank read, the more convinced he became that the knowledge known to mankind today had also been known in the past. How else could the pyramids have been built? How was it possible for electric batteries to have existed several thousand years ago? And then there was the mystery of all mysteries. A three-thousand-year-old Mayan artifact had been found. Made of pure gold, it looked just like a jet plane.

Frank became so absorbed in what he was doing he was startled by the stage manager's voice. "Ten minutes till showtime, Frank."

He never dressed so quickly in his life. Once in his tux, he pulled on his gloves, grabbed his pointer, put on his top hat and cape and rushed to the far corner of the stage. Just in time, too, because the orchestra was already seated. As soon as he heard the resounding clash of cymbals, which was his cue, Frank walked out on stage. As usual the applause was deafening. It gave him an adrenalin rush, a high much stronger than the occasional lines of coke he'd snort. It always did. He was in his element now. He was no longer Frank Santino, a man who only minutes earlier worried about losing his job. He was Santino the Magician, the illusionist extraordinaire, who could summon demons and spirits at will. He could even conjure an image of the devil to appear.

It was almost midnight when Frank pulled his Ferrari inside his garage. He cursed. Why did he step up to that crap table where a high roller had been winning? No sooner had he placed a bet on the pass line, the guy had crapped out. It took him less than five minutes to lose three thousand dollars. What a fool he was.

As usual, Dottie was lounging by the pool, sipping champagne. Her younger brother, Max Hunter, was there, too. He was so different from Dottie that no one would have guessed they were related. Max didn't have much going for him physically. His nose looked as if God had missed his mark when he had placed it on his face. His eyes were set too close together, and he had a skin condition, which made his complexion look like someone had spread death on a soda cracker.

A year or so ago Frank had stumbled upon one of Dottie's old shoe boxes where he found a Bronze Star. Curious, he had asked her about it. She had been reluctant to talk about the medal at first. He finally pried it out of her, but only after he had promised he would never acknowledge to Max he knew about his stint in the Army. It seemed that Max Hunter had more than just a keen mind.

While in the Army, Max had attended a Special Forces Qualification Course. While there, one of the non-commissioned officers discovered that Max excelled at the rifle range. Having been a hunter, his special talent was long distance shooting.

Max had been deployed as a sniper in support of Operation Iraq Freedom several times and that's how he earned the Bronze Star, which had been awarded to him for valor under fire. Had Dottie not told him about Max's tour in the Army, Frank would have never found out he had been credited with seventy-three "kills." Apparently Max was ashamed for being the one responsible for ending so many lives.

To this day Frank had a difficult time believing that a timid, soft-spoken, introverted person like Max had been a decorated war hero. His unusual talent had certainly been well camouflaged. He was a mild-mannered person almost to the point of being meek. Max was the kind of individual who would take a detour around a bug before stepping on it. When Frank had found out about Max's past, he had earned Frank's admiration and respect. Not because he had killed all those people, but because he had risked his life to do so in order that his comrades wouldn't have to suffer the same fate as the enemy.

Funny how things worked out. Max openly worshiped Frank for his talent as an illusionist, even though Frank felt his contribution to society was somewhat trite. On the other hand, Frank secretly admired Max for his bravery. He knew he could never have done what Max did. He never would have had the guts. Max possessed the intelligence to become whatever he wanted to be. His only problem was he lacked focus and self-confidence.

Dottie made no qualms about wanting the materialistic things life had to offer, but not Max. He was more spiritual, more introspective than his sister. Frank also felt sorry for Max. He seemed to be always searching for answers . . . answers, which always eluded him.

Frank walked over and extended his hand. "How have you been?"

"Okay, I guess," Max said rather timidly. "I've almost completed the required course work for my doctorate."

"That's great. Dottie told me you are now majoring in philosophy." Frank had a plan and nothing was going to sway him from accomplishing his objective. "I have a business proposition for you. Are you interested?" He placed an arm around Max and led him to the far side of the pool so Dottie couldn't listen in on their conversation.

Max hesitated. "Would I have to do something illegal?"

"No, no. Of course not, but maybe we should talk inside." Frank steered Max to a richly-appointed den. This was his room, a room Dottie seldom entered. An expensive Persian carpet that Dottie had chosen for him was on the floor. The sofa and chairs were covered in horsehide. They had been specially made for him by a well-known upholsterer. The seats in his Ferrari were made of the same leather. He liked the smell. Frank walked up to the wet bar and poured Max and himself some cognac from a crystal decanter.

Max swirled the amber-colored liquid and took a taste. "Not bad. Not bad at all."

Frank worked at keeping his voice even. "It sure as hell better be good. The stuff is expensive."

Max tried to make himself comfortable in the chair. "You said earlier you had a proposition for me. What do you have in mind?"

Frank took another sip of cognac. "First, I have to ask you some questions. How fluent is your Italian?"

"You already know I can speak the language. That is, if it's Sicilian. I can also read it, but I don't write it too well."

Frank nodded. "I just needed to be sure, that's all. Dottie told me you decided to become a teacher. Is that true?"

Max beamed. It wasn't often Frank had seen him this animated. "A college professor. I want to teach philosophy. I swear to you, Frank. Once I get my doctorate, I'll find a job and then I'll pay back every cent I borrowed from you. I know I'll never make the kind of money you make, but money isn't as important to me as it is to you. Besides, college professors do all right."

The corners of Frank's mouth shaped into a grin. "Relax, Max. I'm here to help you . . . that is, if you are willing to help me." He poured some more cognac into his brother-in-law's snifter. "You said you are studying philosophy, right?"

"I know what you are thinking, but philosophy majors are in high demand right now. With a doctorate in the subject, there would be many—"

Frank cut him off in mid-sentence. "Have you started your dissertation?"

"Not yet. That's why I'm here. I thought maybe you could float me another loan. If I didn't have to work, I could complete a thesis in less than a year."

Frank changed the subject. "Do you know anything about the akashic records?"

"Of course. What philosophy major doesn't?"

Frank didn't want to upset Max, but he had to find out if he was telling the truth. "Can you tell me in plain English what the records stand for?"

Max arched his brows. "When did you become interested in the akashic records?"

"That's not really important. What is important is whether you can define the concept for me in laymen's terms."

Max started to pace the room. "Okay, I'll try. It's not easy to give a person a simple, concise answer. The word 'akashic' postulates the existence of an objective, intellectually-comprehensive spiritual world that's accessible through inner development."

"For heaven's sake, Max. I'd like you to give me an explanation, not a dissertation."

"Sorry. I get a little carried away sometimes. To put it simply, if a person can train his mind, and that is a big if, that person's mind will be able to enter a place that doesn't physically exist."

Frank was about to say something, but Max stopped him. "But you must remember that claims made by those advocating the existence of the akashic records cannot be tested."

"What if I was to tell you there is a book, a very, very special book that can guide the reader to those records?"

Max opened his mouth to speak, but no words came out. Finally, he said, "Are you serious? That would be like proving heaven really exists."

Frank gave some thought to what Max had just said. "That or a hell!"

CHAPTER 8

Cardinal Giuseppe Mercati took big steps as he walked upon the colorful mosaic floor. He had a determined stride, always in a hurry, always with a purpose and when he walked, one could see the flash of his sash and swirling red robe. The splendidly frescoed hall he was passing through was illuminated by large stained-glass windows. Furnished with elaborate hand-carved wooden benches and intricately embroidered silk draperies, the art in the Vatican Library was every bit as impressive as the Raphael tapestries in the Sistine Chapel.

Giuseppe reflected on his meteoric rise to cardinal. He had wanted to become a politician, probably because he had a gift for endearing people to him, but that was not to be. For as long as he could remember, his parents had encouraged him to join the clergy. When he entered the priesthood, his wealthy father urged him to set his sights higher. He told him that with his help, and Giuseppe's uncanny ability of endearing people to him, he would become promoted. Giuseppe also knew that had it not been for his father, he most likely wouldn't be working at the Vatican.

Tall and broad shouldered, he had large warm eyes, which were usually shielded. Their color was brown, veiled down to blackness whenever he was deep in thought. A shock of black hair combed straight back with specks of grey at the temples made him look distinguished. Some would think him handsome were it not for his nose. It appeared to have been pinched in by a pair of strong fingers while still in its formative stage. When he walked, he would do so with his shoulders straight back, head held high. Giuseppe took such long strides that had he had a baton in his hand, one would think he was leading a parade.

For the very last time, Giuseppe stepped into his sumptuous office. He reached inside the drawer of an ancient French writing table which he had used for the better part of seven years, and removed the memorandum with the papal seal.

When the cardinal who had previously been in charge of the Secret Archives died, the pope had appointed him to take his place, a job he was anxious to assume. Now that Giuseppe had been given the assignment, he would be one of only a handful of cardinals who would have immediate access to the pope. This meant there would be a number of clergymen who would be asking him to speak to the pontiff on their behalf. Upon the death of a pope, all cardinals become Cardinal Electors. He hoped this new job would put him in good stead when the conclave met to elect a new pontiff.

In his newly appointed position as Prefect of the Ancient Archives, he would be overseeing the arduous job of sorting though papal records that had been accumulating for centuries. The priests who would be working under his direction, would spend years sifting through the disorganized, poorly catalogued files, but eventually their work would pay off. It would take time, but Giuseppe was confident he could put some order to the place.

A genius when it came to computers, his main job would be to develop a software system capable of logging over a million documents. Most of the information would remain out of reach to all but a privileged few. However, some of the less sensitive, uncontroversial material would be made accessible to outsiders on a limited basis.

The Vatican Library is available to scholars, but only in mitigating circumstances would the pope give his permission for an outsider to enter the Secret Archives. He had heard there was a clandestine chamber somewhere beneath the archives, which he had never seen. He wondered if such a room actually existed and if it did, would his newly appointed position authorize him to enter this very secret place?

With access to the Secret Archives, Giuseppe would be privy to reports of clerics' misbehavior, scandals, usurpations, crimes and sexual pervasions of the most shocking and explosive kind. These were blithely boxed and filed away on thirty miles of shelving among state papers, papal account books as well as an assortment of other documents that belonged to the Church.

As a cardinal, before Giuseppe received his red hat, he had sworn an oath to preserve the secrets of the Church. To outsiders, the furtive material contained within the archives was nothing more than a blank outer wall, an impenetrable maze of archaic titles and unwritten rules, Byzantine in their complexity. But to Giuseppe, this was about to become his life.

Giuseppe had much to be thankful for. At fifty-five years of age, he was one of the most highly respected and influential clerics in Rome. He settled himself in the back seat of the black Chrysler that was always at his disposal. He could have had a Mercedes or virtually any other car of his choice, but he liked American cars and a Cadillac would have brought too much attention.

Giuseppe was one of the few clergymen who had figured out early in life what it would take to become successful and powerful in the hierarchy of the Catholic Church, and more specifically in the Holy See which is the central governing body of the Vatican. Actually, it was a very simple strategy, a creed which he followed religiously. For Giuseppe made himself invisible to those who could not help him rise to the top. He did this so he could spend more time with those who could help him attain a higher position within the clergy.

The drive from Vatican City to the outskirts of Rome would give him a chance to unwind. He planned on attending a party his sister and brother-in-law were giving in his honor at their villa. With his blessing, his sister had married a real estate developer who had close ties with some of the most influential people in Italy. These people not only had the ear of the pope, but they also had the political clout to sway some of his peers, all members of the College of Cardinals, to their way of thinking.

Giuseppe knew the pope would not live much longer. Before the pontiff passed on, he wanted to make certain his brother-in-law had introduced him to all of his friends and business associates. It was so easy. They were all Catholics. What better way to become noticed than to listen to their confessions and then absolve them of their sins.

He figured if he placed himself in front of the right people that eventually his name would come up as a possible successor to the pope. He would be competing for the vote among an elite group of cardinals, but Giuseppe felt he had the edge. He was well connected and came from a prominent Italian family. He had a lot of energy, was charismatic and leaned toward the more conservative views of the Church. And now that the pope had placed him in charge of the Secret Archives, he would become privy to some of the deepest secrets of the Archdiocese.

The black Chrysler followed the serpentine driveway and stopped in front of a port de couch ere. The minute Giuseppe exited the car, he was greeted by his sister, Carlotta. She had a dark perpetual tan that formed quite a contrast against her coal black eyes and pearl-white, evenly-spaced teeth, the kind one usually sees in toothpaste commercials. She was impeccably groomed as usual, wearing a black silk dress with matching pearl earrings and necklace. "You finally got your wish, didn't you, Giuseppe?"

"The pope has entrusted me with a monumental task, and I will do whatever it takes so as not to disappoint His Eminence."

Carlotta hugged him to her. When her mouth was close to his ear, she whispered, "One of these days, you will be the pope."

"If it is God's will, dear sister. If it is God's will." He gently distanced himself from Carlotta. Even though she was his sister, the servants were watching. After all, he was a cardinal.

The two entered the sprawling villa, which her husband, Antonio, bought for Carlotta as a wedding present. An extravagant gift, Giuseppe thought, but then nothing was too good for his sister. Giuseppe believed his much younger sister had a face of an angel. Her smooth skin had a satin sheen to it, and then there were her eyes. Whenever he looked into them, it was as if he was staring into a pair of black, bottomless pools.

Carlotta's husband, Antonio, was in the foyer. Impeccably dressed in a black tuxedo, he was bending the ear of one of the guests. Giuseppe took a glass of grappa from a passing waiter and approached him. "I see you bought Carlotta the villa. I knew that sooner or later, she'd get her way."

Antonio kissed Giuseppe's ring. "Forgive me, Father, for I have sinned."

Giuseppe laughed. Most of the time he laughed out of politeness because Antonio's jokes were seldom funny, but he found this particular retort humorous.

Antonio took Giuseppe's arm. "Come, there are people here you must meet."

CHAPTER 9

Max Hunter was a loner. He had always been a loner, not so much by choice as by circumstances. Both of his parents had died in an automobile accident the summer before his freshman year of high school. There was no insurance and very little money to speak of. Dottie cancelled her plans to attend college and went to work so she could support the two of them. He owed her a debt of gratitude because if she hadn't fought to keep him, he would have ended up being a ward of the state.

Max had been attending high school about a week before he found out why students were tittering behind his back. One day, he mustered up the courage to approach one of them, a senior, and had asked.

"You mean you really don't know?" came the reply. "Your sis works at a tittie bar."

He had refused to believe him. In fact, he had been determined to defend her honor, but the boy was much bigger than he was, and all he got for his effort was a black eye and a bloody nose.

"If you don't believe me, go see for yourself," the boy had told him. "She works at a place called The Pink Pussycat. That's where all the rich guys go to jerk off. The dummy who takes out the trash usually forgets to lock the back door. Kids sneak in there all the time so they can take a peek at the big-boobied chicks."

Max had gone. He got caught sneaking into the place a couple of times, but finally his perseverance had paid off. He had never seen his sister naked before. In fact, whenever she would change clothes, she would always make sure her door was closed. That's why it was so hard for him to internalize the scene he had witnessed at the strip joint. She might as well have been nude because the only thing she had on was a pair of high heels and a string bikini that left nothing to the imagination. Like a snake, she had wrapped herself around a pole. Her mouth was partially open in a suggestive pose; the lipstick so thick you could have scraped it off with a trowel.

He had never confronted her about her job. Maybe it was because he was afraid he would have to go to an orphanage, or maybe it was that he was embarrassed about what she did for a living. He kept pretty much to himself after that. He spent all of his spare time buried in some book. He loved to read. That's probably why he liked school so much.

By the time Max returned to his dingy one-room flat in San Francisco, his head was spinning. Frank had given him a five-thousand-dollar retainer as well as a copy of the forms he had to complete so he could gain admittance to the Vatican Library.

Proving or disproving the existence of the akashic records would be no easy task. In the beginning, Max had been hesitant to take on such a monumental undertaking, but the more he read about the alleged records the more he warmed up to the idea. It would certainly make an interesting topic for a doctoral dissertation. And if there was a shred of truth to the age-old myth, maybe with the grimoire's help, he could prove their existence.

Max understood the main premise. If a person could see his actions from a past life, the experience could help that person attain a higher degree of potential in his present life. More specifically, souls prior to being reincarnated go to a "library" where they get an opportunity to view those pages associated with the new life they are about to undertake. The pages are not sequential because along the course of a person's life, free will can change paths, events, and outcomes. As the soul prepares for a new life with the intent of learning a particular lesson, it will also choose a body that will help it consummate the reincarnation process.

Although Max wasn't convinced it was possible for an old soul to be reborn into a new body, he was also hard pressed to explain déjà vu. It was uncanny why some places he visited for the very first time seemed familiar while other places did not.

After scrutinizing the Vatican's application, he decided the first thing he had to do was develop a plausible hypothesis; one he would attempt to prove. Then he would need to explain the reason or reasons why he was advocating that particular position. Of course, whichever position he chose would have to be supported by facts, and the only way to gather these facts was through research.

Although the akashic records were about as intangible as clouds in the sky, Max decided to prove their existence; a topic no scholar had ever attempted to tackle. He weighed the pros and cons of such a difficult undertaking. If he wasn't able to prove his hypothesis, he would be washed out of the doctoral program. He had failed to complete a dissertation two other times, and this was his last chance. If he didn't obtain one this time, he could forget about ever becoming a college professor. With only a master's degree, he'd be lucky to get a job teaching high school.

There was another problem. He would be tackling a difficult, controversial topic, one in which the Archdiocese didn't believe in, namely reembodiment. Proposing to prove a theory that dealt with rebirth would be risky. Unless the person reviewing his request was able to maintain a sense of objectivity, his application would most likely be denied. However, if he could prove the records actually existed, he could end up winning the Pulitzer Prize. Although he was proposing to tackle an extremely difficult topic, even for the most experienced researcher, he decided to forge ahead. He couldn't very well back out now, not when Frank had already agreed to provide him with the financial backing he so desperately needed. And the last thing he wanted to do was to let his brother-in-law down.

Max honed the application to perfection. All that was left was to give the Vatican a reason for wanting to tackle such an ambitious topic. He wrestled with the response for quite some time, but finally came up with the verbiage he thought the Vatican would accept. Just as he finished putting his thoughts down on paper, the phone rang. He instantly recognized Frank's voice.

"How are you coming along with the application?"

"I was just getting ready to send it off."

"Sorry, but there is something you need to include. I had meant to give it to you when you were here, but I forgot."

"What's that?"

"It's a letter I bought from an antiquarian bookseller."

"Why do you think it should be included?"

"Because it proves the Vatican has *The Testament of Solomon*, that's why. They may very well refuse your request, but they won't be able to claim they don't have that particular grimoire."

"Clever. You are one shrewd guy, you know that?"

Frank laughed. "Listen, I'm Catholic and I know what those priests can be like. Since you don't have a fax, I'll scan the letter and email it to you."

"There is something you need to know," Max said.

"Don't tell me you decided not to do it."

"No. No. Quite the contrary," Max said. "Once I began researching the akashic records, I made the decision to write a doctoral dissertation on the subject."

"Glad to hear it," Frank replied. "Now you'll also need the grimoire."

When Max had disconnected the phone, he realized Frank was right. If he didn't obtain *The Testament of Solomon*, it would be difficult, if not impossible, to prove the existence of the akashic records. He decided he would have to lay his hands on every scrap of information that dealt with the knowledge of the ancients. When he read about the scientific revolution, he was shocked to learn that the brilliant scientists of the day were convinced they were merely rediscovering scientific principles of the past, and that the vast body of pristine knowledge of the ancients was somehow lost and forgotten. Could they have been wrong? Max didn't think so.

Maybe, just maybe the ancients knew the age-old questions Max had been asking himself ever since he could remember. Who are we, where did we come from, and why are we here? Max turned off the computer and leaned back in his chair. If the Vatican gave him permission to read the grimoire, would he find the answers there?

CHAPTER 10

Cardinal Giuseppe Mercati woke up with a headache. He had promised himself not to stay too late at his sister's house. But he had lost all track of time once his brother-in-law began to introduce him to his guests. They were people who held prominent positions in Rome. The mayor, the chief of police, a few industrialists, a number of bankers and even a prominent senator. The grappa had been excellent, and his only regret was that he had drunk too much of it.

Since Giuseppe was partial to grappa, a waiter was always nearby with a glass. There were so many people to meet. The best part of it was they all wanted a piece of him. Before he left, Antonio had pulled him aside. "We're grooming you to become the next pope, you know."

"And just how are you going to do that?" Giuseppe already knew the answer, but he wanted to hear what Antonio had to say.

"Are you kidding? I've talked to numerous people whom you've met. They are all anxious to invite you into their homes."

"And what did you say?" Giuseppe had asked.

"They wanted to know if you would come. I informed them that you were an extremely busy man." Antonio grinned. "I also told them you enjoy going to parties and if they gave you ample notice, you'd be delighted. I told our guests you have the pope's ear. The feedback Carlotta and I received was extremely positive. People always want to back a winner, you know. You're young for a cardinal, Italian, and come from a good family. You are also witty, charming, and politically astute."

"I appreciate very much that you and my sister are in my corner, but please be careful of what you say. Sometimes, if you give people too much information, they end up using it against you."

Antonio's eyes widened. "But you are a man of God. Why would anyone wish you harm?"

Giuseppe was amazed at how naïve Antonio could be. "It makes no difference. There are other cardinals who would like to become pope. Many are on a quest to get votes. When you tell people that I have the pope's ear, some might think I am a braggart, which I am not."

"Okay, lesson learned. I get your point. But just you wait and see. These people will include you into their inner circle. After all, everyone who's rich wants to know a cardinal who is as close to the pope as you are, a dying one at that."

Giuseppe didn't have time to muse anymore about the party. He dressed with great care for His Eminence had requested to see him. A messenger had informed him to come by the Holy Father's private quarters following the seven o'clock morning Mass.

Two pontifical Swiss Guards stood at attention when Giuseppe approached the papal apartment. Each was holding a tall lance. Giuseppe always thought their uniforms looked ludicrous. He had to admit the blue, red and yellow stripes were colorful, but the flared trousers and sleeves were over the top. Once he was a few feet away from the portal, they snapped their lances against their sides. At that moment, a young priest opened an inner door. "His Eminence is awaiting you, Cardinal Mercati. Would you follow me, please?"

With the exception of the paintings on the walls, the papal apartment was sparsely furnished, and very modern. This always surprised Giuseppe as each pope had at his disposal priceless treasures, all gifts from leaders of countries throughout the world. For the Holy See is more than just the central government of the Church. It is recognized by international law as a sovereign entity with which diplomatic relations can be maintained.

One of the warehouses he'd once seen was full of heavily-adorned Baroque furniture, rich fabrics, frescoes, priceless paintings as well as bronze and alabaster statues. Most popes chose to place many of their gifts in the Vatican Museum and this pope was no exception. Because there wasn't enough room in the Museum to display all the treasure, it was kept in several large underground storehouses the Vatican had built.

When a new pope was elected by the College of Cardinals, he would decide what objects he wanted displayed in the papal apartment. Some popes left such decisions to others, but Giuseppe knew if he were to be chosen that he'd decorate the spacious rooms to his own taste, which his sister claimed was impeccable. Unlike this pope, he would want to surround his living quarters with numerous paintings and antiques as most of them were priceless.

The pope was sitting in a chair upholstered in a rich burgundy fabric. He looked pale, the skin almost translucent. His eyes were watery, and he was having some difficulty breathing. An oxygen tank was by his side. The minute Giuseppe entered the room, he rushed to kneel in front of the Holy Father. He kissed the papal ring which was not that much larger than his own. The pope was wearing a simple, unadorned white robe. A golden cross attached to a braided gold chain dangled from his neck.

"Please, we can dispense with formality in my quarters," he said in a voice devoid of vitality. The pope waved Giuseppe to a seat not far from his chair. After they had spent a few minutes talking about things of little consequence, the pope pointed to a box resting on the mantle.

"Go and open it," he said. "I want you to take what is inside." Giuseppe opened the lid to the ornate box that was encrusted with semi-precious jewels. Inside was a large iron key the size of a handgun.

"Do you know what this is?" the Holy Father asked.

"No, Your Eminence. I do not."

"Now that you're responsible for the Secret Archives, this key is yours. Only two exist—one I have; the other is this one. The key unlocks a door to a room underneath the Secret Archives. Some have called it the 'Room of Dark Secrets.' Although there are many who speculate that such a room exists, no one except popes and cardinals who had been entrusted with the responsibility of keeping our Church's secrets safe from intruders have ever been inside. The room is rather small, but some of the information it contains is so vile that my predecessors and I have excluded the material from the Secret Archives."

Guiseppe made eye contact with the pope. "Why not destroy them?" he asked.

A shadow of a smile appeared on the pope's face. "For posterity, Cardinal. For the sake of preserving the history of the Church. They remain stored in boxes, hidden from view in that room. Some of the material is over a thousand years old." The pope gave Giuseppe a penetrating look. "You must promise me you will keep them safe."

"I will, Holy Father. I will."

"As you become familiar with the archives, you will most likely place other documents and manuscripts in that room, but you are to never remove anything from it without my permission. Is that understood?"

"Yes, Your Eminence. I understand perfectly."

The key felt heavy in Giuseppe's pocket, but that was not the only thing that weighed on him. He had just been charged by the pope himself to guard the Church's innermost secrets. He readily accepted both the responsibility and the prestige that came with his new job.

CHAPTER 11

On the day Cardinal Giuseppe Mercati had been appointed Prefect of the Secret Archives, Cardinal Oservatore Romanus had been placed in charge of the Vatican Library. Romanus was pleased that the pope had picked him to take Cardinal Mercati's place as the Library's prefect. Unlike Mercati, Romanus did not have a life outside the Church. Because he sincerely believed God controlled his destiny, Romanus didn't dwell much on diplomacy. He stated his thoughts clearly and bluntly; however, they were usually tempered with humor.

Cardinal Romanus was the antithesis of Cardinal Mercati. Where Mercati had come from Italian aristocracy, Romanus came from a lower middle-class family. His parents had both died toiling the earth when Romanus was quite young, and he spent his boyhood years living in a Catholic orphanage. Physically, the two cardinals were also quite different. Mercati was tall and had good posture while Romanus was short. His shoulders were rounded, and when he walked, he did so with his knees and elbows akimbo, and with his head down. In fact, the only remarkable feature about Cardinal Romanus were his eyebrows. Arched and bushy, they were the color of cumulous clouds and rested high above his eyes. Their appearance looked somewhat incongruous to his bald, shiny head.

Where Cardinal Mercati was at ease with Rome's elite, Cardinal Romanus only felt comfortable among the clergy. He liked to think of himself as a simple man whose only purpose in life was to serve God, the pope, and his beloved Church.

Romanus decided his first order of business would be to remodel his office. He thought the antique writing table was too small and the wallpaper with the flowery prints too feminine. Several carpenters were making so much noise with their hammers that he felt a headache coming on. He needed to get out of his place of work. He headed toward the Sistine Hall, one of the most beautiful features of the Library. Romanus always experienced a sense of peace as he passed through this vestibule on his way to the many rooms that contained a million or so bound books. Some said the hall's Baroque statues, murals, frescoes and finely-carved marble pillars were the finest in the world. On the far side of the hall, Romanus stopped to examine the most famous book in the Christian world. The handwritten manuscript was housed in a glass case not only fireproof, but also impervious to theft. Codex Vaticanus Graecus was the oldest-known, nearly-complete bible. Dating back to the fourth century, it was written in Greek on seven hundred fifty-nine vellum leaves. Of course Romanus knew all this, but always valued the connection it gave him to the past.

By the time he returned to his office, the workmen were gone. In place of wallpaper, the rich wood paneling he had requested gave the room a masculine look. Just when he thought he would be able to work in solitude, one of the many priests who handled requests to peruse the Library's books approached him. "Normally I wouldn't bother you with such matters, but an American student who attends the University of San Francisco has asked if he could take a look at one of our grimoires. It's called *The Testament of Solomon.*"

"What's so special about the request?"

The priest handed Romanus not only the application, but what was attached to it as well.

"What's this?" Romanus asked, as he examined the facsimile of the document enclosed with the paperwork. Then he proceeded to answer his own question. "It looks like a letter of gratitude that was written in the seventeenth century." Romanus scrutinized the paper. "It's from a cardinal. His name is rather difficult to make out, but I think it's from Cardinal Cervini. Did you check this out?"

"Yes, Your Eminence. I have already taken the liberty to make sure it's not a forgery. The handwriting is that of the cardinal. He was the Library's prefect from 1629 until 1648."

Cardinal Romanus took a few minutes to read through Max Hunter's application. "He certainly chose an interesting topic, don't you think?"

"Yes, Your Eminence."

"Then what's the problem? You have the authority to either grant or deny his request."

"Unfortunately, we can't find the grimoire he wants."

Romanus leaned forward in his chair. "What do you mean, you can't find it?"

"I did locate a ledger. This particular grimoire was a gift from the Ribaldi family. It was logged in on July 12, 1602.

"Yes. Go on, go on."

"All I can tell you is the grimoire is missing."

"I know that, young man," Romanus said gruffly. "But the letter states it was found."

"That's true. But there is no record of the book's title anywhere. I checked the central processing unit. I also looked for the name in the card catalogue files that as yet have not been entered into the computer. I even looked for the reference in the indices that are dedicated to manuscripts. That's why I thought I should bring the matter to your attention. Without an index card, even if the grimoire is here, there would be no way of finding it."

Romanus hadn't been at his new job for even a day and already there was a problem. "I want you to make sure. Look through the card catalogues again. Maybe the book is alphabetically listed in the 'S' section, the 'S' standing for Solomon. Did you look for it there?"

"I have," the priest said.

Romano's voice softened. "Tell me, was the grimoire published or was it written by hand?"

"I really don't know. Does that make a difference?"

Romanus wondered if all the priests who worked in the Library were as naïve as this one. "If the grimoire in question has been published after 1501, we're out of luck. But what if it's among the 'incunabula'?"

The priest's eyes lit up. "Of course. Why didn't I think of that? We have approximately eight thousand five hundred books that were printed prior to 1501. And you are right. The book could very well be among those we refer to as the incunabula."

Romanus was quick to dispense some additional advice. "I want to remind you that no handwritten books would be in that section, even if they had been dated prior to 1501."

I'll get on it right away," the priest said.

Several days passed. Cardinal Romanus was so caught up in his newly assigned duties that he all but forgot about the grimoire when the priest came to see him. "I'm afraid the news is not good, Your Eminence. I found a reference book that contains information about *The Testament of Solomon*. This particular grimoire was not published. It was written by hand."

"That is unfortunate." Romanus thanked the priest and dismissed him. Alone in his office, he contemplated his next move. The simple thing to do would be to deny Max Hunter's request and place the entire matter out of his mind. The chances of someone else wanting to access that particular grimoire was virtually negligible. But his conscience wouldn't allow him to do that. The pope had just entrusted him with this assignment, and to skirt the issue of a missing book wouldn't make for a good beginning.

Romanus knew the Secret Archives, which were now headed by Cardinal Mercati, had been formed in the early part of the eighteenth century. In those days, the word "secret" meant the pope's own. All books, manuscripts and correspondence considered to be either controversial in nature, seditious or contentious to the Church were removed from the Vatican Library and placed in the Secret Archives. Could *The Testament of Solomon* be there?

He again called in the priest who had brought the matter of the missing grimoire to his attention and asked him to locate the records of the transfer. Twenty-six thousand six hundred items had been initially moved, but *The Testament of Solomon* was not among them. That didn't surprise Romanus. Typically, grimoires didn't contain information sensitive enough to be placed in the Secret Archives. Most dealt with recipes for formulas, potions and elixirs that would heal the sick. Some even revealed how to perform magical tricks. Only a handful dealt with mysticism and the occult; intonations supposedly powerful enough to resurrect demons and angels from the spiritual world. Could *The Testament of Solomon* be one of those?

Romanus reread the copy of the letter that thanked Archbishop Alberto Dominique for returning the grimoire to its rightful place. The letter was written in May of 1637. Since the Secret Archives hadn't come into existence till 1744, the stolen grimoire had to have been returned to the Vatican Library. If the grimoire wasn't in the Library and hadn't been transferred to the Secret Archives, then where could it be?

CHAPTER 12

Frank Santino was not a patient man. Three weeks had passed and still no word from the Vatican. Frank decided it was time to take matters into his own hands. He remembered that the antiquarian bookseller had told him a man by the name of Jonathan Hollingsworth owned the other grimoire. Although Los Angeles was a big city, Hollingsworth's residence would not be that hard to find. Unfortunately, the wealthy industrialist's telephone number wasn't listed. So Frank did the next best thing. He wrote Hollingsworth a letter requesting to see *The Testament of Solomon*. He also told him he had recently purchased an ancient piece of correspondence that made a specific reference to the book. His reasoning was that Hollingsworth would most likely want the letter as it would provide further evidence as to the legitimacy of his book. Frank decided he would use the letter as ammunition. He would give it to Hollingsworth provided the man would let him spend some time with the grimoire.

The telephone call came four days later. The voice was female and seemed tentative. "Hello. I'm looking for Frank Santino."

Thinking it was one of his fans who had acquired his unlisted number, he had almost hung up. Instead, he answered in an even voice. "This is Frank Santino."

"My name is Laura Hollingsworth. Are you the person who inquired about that book? I believe it's called *The Testament of Solomon*."

It was as if an electric current had coursed through him. His heart was beating so fast he was having trouble enunciating his words. "Yes, Mrs. Hollingsworth. I'm the one who wrote your husband the letter."

"He is not my husband. I'm his daughter."

"Sorry. But yes, I would very much like to see the book. I also have a letter that refers to it. I thought your father might be—"

"I'm afraid that won't be possible," Laura Hollingsworth cut in. "Ever since my father purchased the book, he's been acting strange. He spends days with it, alone. He locks himself in the den and rarely bothers to come out. It's gotten so bad he doesn't even bother to open his mail. The reason I'm calling is because I wanted to ask you if you know what's in the book."

Frank did not want to tell a bold-face lie, so he decided to stretch the truth. "I might be able to help."

There was an awkward moment of silence. Frank knew if he said anything else it might do more harm than good. Finally, in a little more than a whisper, Laura Hollingsworth replied, "I'd like to hear what you have to say. What's best for you, morning or afternoon?"

Frank was overcome with joy. Maybe he wouldn't get a chance to see the book, but at least this was a start. "Mornings are best for me. I could take a flight out of Vegas and be in L.A. by nine. Would ten o'clock tomorrow suit you?"

"Ten o'clock would be fine. I assume you have the address."

"Yes."

"I'll leave word with the guard. And Mr. Santino?"

"Yes."

"I want you to make me a promise. In the event you see my father, which is unlikely, promise you won't mention the book."

* * *

The flight to Los Angeles was uneventful and the house had been easy to find. Actually, it looked more like a museum than a private residence. Sprawled over several acres, the home was located in Holmby Hills, considered to be one of the most prestigious areas in L.A. The gatehouse alone was larger than an average-sized home.

When Frank identified himself, the two massive wrought-iron gates swung open to reveal a paved driveway that led to the main house. It reminded him of one of the wings at the Louvre. Constructed out of grey granite, it had a gabled copper roof that had partially turned green with age. He came to a stop in front of a majestic fountain that spewed jets of water from four brass dolphins. No sooner had he opened the car door than a man wearing a butler's suit greeted him. "Mr. Santino, if you would please follow me. Miss Hollingsworth has been expecting you."

Frank heard the chanting the minute he entered the house. He was fairly certain it was coming from a room down the hall. The words sounded muffled as if the person mouthing them was doing so through a piece of cloth. The butler left and he was alone. He strained his ears in the hope he could make out some of the words, but the chanting had stopped.

Then he saw her. She was walking down the carpeted stairs. Although one of her delicate hands was on the wooden balustrade, it didn't appear she was using the railing for support. The woman looked frail, maybe it was because her face was so pale. He took her to be in her mid-thirties, but she looked older than her years. Maybe it was the style of her hair. It was pulled up in a bun just like his mother used to wear. A shawl with tassels was wrapped around her slim shoulders. It draped down to the waist of her ankle-length dress.

"You must be Mr. Santino," she said barely above a whisper.

He walked toward the stairs to shake her hand. "Miss Hollingsworth. Thank you for seeing me."

"Please call me Laura. My father is indisposed at the moment. He is in the den with that cursed book again. Ever since he purchased it some four months ago, he hasn't been himself. He locks himself up with it for hours at a time. You can probably hear him now repeating certain phrases over and over again. Most of the words are Italian, but they make absolutely no sense to me."

Laura led Frank into a living room the size of a gymnasium. Although someone had started a fire in the two massive fireplaces, which were on opposite sides of the room, Frank could still feel an icy draft.

"Please, won't you have a seat?" Laura said.

Suddenly, a chill coursed through him. It was as if someone had placed a block of ice at the back of his neck. As soft as a brush, a current of air touched his face, but quite possibly it was just his imagination because the massive French doors that led to the patio were closed.

"Tell me. What do you know about this book . . . this grimoire?" Laura asked.

Frank felt sorry for the woman, and he didn't even know why. He decided it would be best to tell her what he knew without embellishing the story.

"I talked to the person here in Los Angeles who sold the book to your father. Actually, I believe he told me he brokered the sale. He thought there were only two such books in existence. Your father has one and the Vatican has the other. The bookseller seemed to know a great deal about this particular grimoire. He told me grimoires written by hand are quite rare, and this one was supposedly copied from an even older grimoire that King Solomon had written."

"Why do you want the book?" Laura asked.

"The bookseller told me this particular grimoire can teach a person how to use his mind to perform extraordinary feats. I'm a magician, and I wanted it so I could learn how to move objects around the room." Frank hesitated. "Do you mind my asking why your father bought the book?"

"He collects first editions, rare manuscripts and the like. Has been for years. There are probably over a thousand in his library. For some reason, this book has become very special to him. I say this because I've hardly ever seen him take notice of the others."

"So you say this book is different?"

"He recites words and phrases out of it constantly. Sometimes I hear him repeating the unfamiliar words well into the night." A worried expression crossed her face. "I'm a little frightened to tell you the truth. At first, he just appeared to be interested in the book. Now, he's obsessed with it. He can't seem to tear himself away from it. And it's getting worse. With the exception of taking a short break for meals, he spends all of his waking hours with that damned book. He doesn't even bother to leave the house anymore. In fact, he hardly even acknowledges my presence. It's as if he's become possessed. And there is something else, something I can't quite put my finger on."

Laura placed her hands against her face and began to cry. Then she wiped away the tears. "I'm sorry. I don't even know you, and here I am making a fool of myself. But I thought you might know why he is acting so peculiar."

"I can't say that I do. You said there was something else."

"Yes. I know you will probably think I have an overactive imagination, but ever since he purchased that cursed grimoire, I've felt a presence in the house."

"Do you sometimes feel a cold draft?" Frank asked.

"Yes, but how did you know?"

"I felt it, too. Just a few minutes ago. It was as if someone placed something very cold against the back of my neck."

"Oh my goodness! And I thought I was imagining it."

This was the opening Frank had been looking for, so he took it. "I wish I could help. Maybe if you could let me take a look at the book, I could—"

She was quick to interrupt. "Oh, I couldn't do that! Maybe I could have when he first purchased it, but now he won't even let me come near it." A look of pure horror crossed her face. "Do you think the book might be cursed?"

Frank was quick to reply. "Of course not. It's only a book. It might be old. It might even contain information that enables a person to perform feats of magic, but I can assure you it's harmless." Frank wished he could take back the words. Ever since he had set foot in this house, he wasn't sure of anything anymore.

His words appeared to have a calming effect because Laura said, "Thank you, Mr. Santino. I feel better after talking to you."

Frank rose. "Well, I better be going. I'd like you to take my card. My home and cell numbers are on it. If I can be of further help, don't hesitate to call." He opened the front door. "If I were you, I'd call a physician. You have a family doctor, I assume?"

"Yes, of course."

"I'd have him come by and check your father out. He probably isn't sick. This might be just a phase he's going through, but the doctor might be able to prescribe a medication to calm his nerves."

She waved to him from the doorstep. "I think that's good advice."

On his way back to Vegas, Frank could think of little else except the grimoire. He just knew this had to be a special book or why else would Laura Hollingsworth's father be so obsessed with it?

His only hope now was Max. He needed that Vatican approval. It wouldn't be as good as having his own copy, but it would be better than nothing.

CHAPTER 13

Once Cardinal Oservatore Romanus realized that the grimoire was not in the Vatican Library, he made an appointment to meet with Cardinal Giuseppe Mercati. He had been kept waiting for over a half an hour, which gave him more than enough time to dwell on the man he came to see. To say he didn't much care for Mercati was an understatement. Now seventy-two, Romanus had become a cardinal when he was sixty-three years of age. He was dedicated to serving the Church and unlike Mercati, he had no aspirations of becoming a pope.

Romanus didn't like the idea that a man seventeen years his junior had been appointed as Prefect of the Secret Archives, a post considered by many to be more important than his own. Nonetheless, he had been pleased when the pope had asked him to take the job as Prefect of the Vatican Library. It was an important assignment and one he planned to fulfill to the very best of his ability. After all, the Vatican Library has a special character. Maybe it didn't contain reports dealing with dirty deeds, but it did include secular works and books on theology and canon law. Above all, it housed the purest of the Greek and Latin classics anyone could find.

Romanus was proud of the fact that the Vatican Library had once been a center of the revival of classical culture known as the Renaissance. True, Mercati was responsible for guarding some of the Church's secrets, but to say his job was more important was pure nonsense. In his mind, Romanus felt the only reason Mercati took the job was because the position enabled him to gain access to the pope.

Romanus compared Mercati to a shooting star. He had rapidly come out of obscurity to his current position because he knew the right people, important people. But Romanus was of the opinion that Mercati didn't have the inner spiritual strength to become a pontiff. And, just like a shooting star, he would end up fading into obscurity. For Romanus believed that sooner or later, his peers would recognize him for what he really was—an opportunist who was using political favors to try and worm his way to the top of the archdiocese's food chain. Romanus was sure Mercati had placed his assets either in his sister's name or in the family trust because a man like him wouldn't be willing to relinquish his wealth to the Church. Rumor had it that his father had not only inherited a fortune, but had made several himself.

Romanus crossed himself. He knew it was beneath him to feel such animosity toward any human being, much less a clergyman. He prayed that God would help him push aside his hostility toward a fellow cardinal.

A deep throaty voice roused Romanus from his thoughts. "Oservatore, how are you? So sorry to have kept you waiting, but I had been trying to see His Eminence."

Romanus did not like to be called by his first name, particularly by the likes of this man. "How is the Holy Father?" he asked out of politeness.

"I wish I could tell you he is feeling better. I was told he was too weak to talk. I spoke to one of his doctors who told me all they can do now is try and make him comfortable."

"I'm sorry to hear that," Romanus said sincerely. "I shall pray for His Holiness."

Giuseppe changed the subject. "What brings you here? I suppose you probably have questions about your new post."

"Actually, I don't." It gave Romanus great pleasure to speak those words, not wanting to add more reason for Mercati to feel superior to him. "I came here because a book is missing, and I was hoping you might be able to provide me with some clues as to how I could go about locating it."

* * *

Giuseppe paused for a moment and then placed his arm around Romanus. "Come. Let's go to my office where you can tell me about it."

After Giuseppe had listened to Romanus, he skimmed the copy of the letter Cardinal Cervini had written over four hundred years ago praising Archbishop Dominique for locating the book. He took the letter and walked over to the Xerox machine. "Mind if I make a copy?"

"Of course not," came the reply.

"I must assume the grimoire in question had either been lost or stolen, but according to this letter, it had been returned to the Vatican Library."

"That's what I thought, but one of my assistants checked out every possibility. I even thought the manuscript might have been transferred to the Secret Archives; however, of the twenty-six thousand documents that were moved, there was no mention of *The Testament of Solomon* on the manifest."

Giuseppe figured he wouldn't be able to find an elephant in the room upon room of boxes that were stacked upon one another in the ancient archives, much less a grimoire. But he wasn't about to tell Romanus that. Instead, he chose to humor him. "As you know, record-keeping wasn't all that efficient in the seventeenth and eighteenth centuries. It is quite possible the grimoire is among the original documents that were transferred from the Vatican Library to this place. I would be willing to venture that some books were most likely excluded from the manifest. An oversight by some careless cleric, I'm sure. Here is what I'll do. I have almost completed a software program I've been working on. Once it's finished my staff will begin inserting all the material housed in the Secret Archives into the computer. I will have them be on the lookout for the grimoire. If they find it, you shall be the first to know."

Romanus made an effort to sound sincere. "Thank you, Cardinal. I knew I could count on you."

When Romanus left, Giuseppe glanced at his watch. It was almost five, time to shower and change. He had accepted an invitation from an investment banker who had a summer home in Rome. Antonio and Carlotta had also been invited. This was yet another opportunity to meet powerful, prominent people, people who were in a position to exert their influence over a number of cardinals who would soon be casting a vote for a new pope.

* * *

Cardinal Romanus knew Cardinal Mercati had merely been posturing. He had no intention of looking for the grimoire. After all, didn't he have more important things to do like solicit votes from those who would soon be charged with the responsibility of electing a new pope?

Romanus returned to his office in a foul mood. He had wasted far too much time waiting to see Mercati. He also had a job to do, an important job and the grimoire had already taken up far too much of his time. Romanus didn't want to lie, but in this instance, he didn't know what else to do. After all, he couldn't very well tell an applicant that the Vatican had lost the very book he had requested to see. Romanus called in one of the priests who had the authority to grant requests to conduct research at the Library. After riffling through his desk, he found Max Hunter's application and handed it to him. "I want you to deny this request."

"What shall I state for a reason?" the priest asked.

"Why don't you just say the topic is frivolous and not worthy of academic research. Sign my name to it, if you like."

CHAPTER 14

It was only with a great deal of effort that Frank Santino could finish his last performance. Max had told him earlier he had been denied access to the grimoire because the Vatican felt the request had been frivolous. Frank was angrier with himself than with Max. He should have had a contingency plan to fall back on. Now, he only had six weeks to come up with an engaging show or at least one that would impress Richard Stover and those cohorts he hung around with at the Boulevardier.

When Frank got home, he discovered that Dottie had gone off to some party, but what difference did that make? Frank hadn't told her about the trouble he was in because he knew he couldn't count on her for a solution. He could hear her now. "Oh, honey, I know you. You'll think of something." Think of something! Think of what?

He spent a restless night. Although he was awake when Dottie crawled into bed, he pretended he was asleep. He finally drifted off before dawn. When he woke up, Dottie was no longer in the house. He glanced at his watch. Nine o'clock. He was sure his mentor, Ron Erickson, would be awake. Ron had taught him everything he knew about creating illusions. He had been the best in the business. Maybe, just maybe, the old man had a trick or two he hadn't told him. It had been so long since they talked that Frank had to look up his number.

"Hi, Ron. Frank Santino here. I hope I'm not calling too early."

"Not at my age, you're not. Hell, I've been up for hours. What's up, Frankie?"

Frank hated to be called Frankie, but with Ron he always let it pass. "I'd really like to talk to you. Would you mind if I came to see you?"

"Of course not, but don't you have a show to do?"

"There is no show today. It's Monday."

"Jeez, that's right. You know at my age I have trouble keeping track of time. It seems like one day just flows into another. Just wait till you're eighty-three. You'll know what I mean."

Frank had no illusions about living that long. "I can catch a flight and be at your house in a couple of hours, three at most. Is it okay if I stay the night?"

"Come on down. I would love the company."

When Ron retired, he had purchased a home on the outskirts of Phoenix. Frank caught the first available flight, rented a car and after spending half an hour looking for the residence, pulled up in front of his house. Ron's landscaping consisted of green gravel and a couple of cacti. The house was in need of repair. The stucco had a number of cracks and the paint was peeling off the front door.

Frank was shocked when he saw the retired magician. His wrinkled skin, the color of dried figs, hung loosely on his bony frame. Although Ron looked withered, his eyes still possessed the same sparkle. As if reading Frank's mind, Ron said, "See what you have to look forward to?"

"I'll never make it to your age," Frank replied. "I drink too much."

Ron pointed to a leather chair that had definitely seen better days. "Take the load off; relax. Can I get you a beer?"

"It's too early for that." After the two had reminisced about the past, Frank broached the subject. "What can you tell me about levitation and telekinesis?"

Ron ran one of his hands through his thinning white hair. "Are you thinking about changing the routine?"

Frank did not want to tell his tutor the truth, so he skirted the issue. "I heard there's a magician in France who can move objects around the stage. I was also told he can hang suspended in midair."

"His name is Jacques Lapinè."

"You know him?" Frank asked, somewhat surprised.

"I know of him."

"I don't suppose you know how he manages it?"

"No, but it has to be in one of two ways. He either does it acoustically or electromagnetically."

"You've lost me, Ron. Are you telling me what he does isn't real magic?"

"I think what you really want to know is if what he does is paranormal. The answer is no. Jacques makes people believe he has the ability to conduct paranormal activities when in reality what he does can be explained scientifically."

"Do you mean to tell me there is a scientific basis for what he does?"

"Of course. Let me explain it to you this way. Acoustic telekinesis can be used to suspend matter by using radiation pressure, which comes by creating intense sound waves that cannot be heard by the human ear. The method is difficult to control and there are limits as to how much can be lifted, but certainly a few kilograms would not be that difficult to accomplish."

"So what you are saying is that by controlling these sound waves, the objects appear to float at different heights in a room."

"Exactly," Ron said. "Jacques uses technology just like you do. The difference is in his equipment. It's much more expensive than yours, but then it is also a great deal more sophisticated."

"You mentioned electromagnetic levitation. How does that work?"

Ron scratched the stubble underneath his chin. "Believe it or not, it's one of the oldest levitation techniques. It's far too complicated for me to explain, but I do know its user relies on electromagnetic radiation. I don't think the system would work from a practical sense. First of all, the special coils needed are very expensive as they must be energized by a radio frequency power supply. Also, they wouldn't be portable."

Frank was amazed at Ron's knowledge. "How in the world do you know all this stuff?"

"In order to succeed as a magician, at least over the long haul, one must continually search for new tricks. I had thought about doing levitation acts with small animals. It's been tried before, you know. The problem is the gear can run into an awful lot of money. Most of the equipment I mentioned earlier has to be built into the stage and hidden from view. It isn't something you'd want to lug around with you, I can tell you that. I bet you if Jacques Lapinè can actually levitate, he does so only in one location."

Frank now realized why Stover had given him a chance to come up with a new act. It wasn't out of a sense of loyalty or obligation. Stover just didn't want to spend anymore of the casino's money than he had to. "What if someone came up with a way to move objects around a room without the use of science?" Frank asked.

Ron thought about the question for a moment before responding. "You mean metaphysical levitation? The spiritualists tend to interpret this type of levitation as the supernatural action of a God. A few Yoga masters claim such levitation can and does occur, but only if a person has the ability to enter higher levels of consciousness, such as mystical rapture or astral projection."

"You are talking mind control here, aren't you?" Frank asked.

"I suppose a person has to use mind control to enter into the kind of trance required to lift objects off the ground. It seems to be a very pervasive belief among major world religions that the human mind can be trained to do remarkable things, if a person has the right tools."

Frank had gone full circle and was now back where he had started. He didn't have the money or the expertise to put together an act using either acoustic or electromagnetic levitation. And he didn't know enough about parapsychology to train his mind in order to perform feats that would defy gravity. Things didn't look good for him to stay at the Boulevardier.

On the plane back to Vegas, he decided the only thing he could do was contact his agent and ask him to put out some feelers to see if there were some smaller theater owners out there who would be interested in what he does best—demonical apparitions. The pay would be much less and he and Dottie would most likely have to move, but so what? Dottie would bitch and complain, but if she wanted to stay on the gravy train, she'd have little choice but to go with him.

CHAPTER 15

Giuseppe had been at his new job for a week before he found the time to thoroughly explore both the Secret Archives and the Room of Dark Secrets. In and of themselves, the Secret Archives were anything but impressive. Just a massive repository with shelves that contained books, manuscripts, as well as correspondence that the popes throughout history had held dear to them. He knew the first thing he needed to do was organize the material in a way that it could be retrieved. Unfortunately, the Dewey Decimal System, which was the system almost all libraries used, wouldn't work.

Giuseppe came up with a unique, simple approach. He divided the archives into two sections. The first section would house all records prior to the Napoleonic War and records after this war would be placed in the second section. Then he divided each of those two sections into four major categories: books and manuscripts were to be placed on lower shelves so they could easily be reached while correspondence dealing with clerics' misdeeds and sensitive communication written by popes, cardinals and archbishops or other administrators of the Holy See would be located on the upper shelves.

Giuseppe knew the work would continue for quite some time. He told his staff that prior to making an entry into the computer, every document had to be reviewed. If it was felt the file was no longer time sensitive and could be declassified, he wanted to make the final decision himself. And, if he agreed, he would forward it to Cardinal Romanus at the Vatican Library where it would be logged in and stored.

It took some time for Giuseppe to find the Room of Dark Secrets. It was beneath the building that contained the Secret Archives, but to get to it, he had to pass through a dimly-lit underground tunnel he was positive hadn't been used often.

Finally, after he had taken two wrong turns, he came upon a massive wooden door. He could tell it was very old because the oak beams were held together by large iron nails that obviously had been forged by hand. The locking mechanism was also ancient. He fully expected to have some trouble unlocking such an antique security device. But no sooner had he inserted the massive key than he heard a resounding click, and the lock that had held the door firmly in place gave way. He gently leaned again the door and it swung open. He groped around for a light switch and found it near the doorjamb. The cavern-like room was illuminated by a number of light bulbs, which hung loosely from the ceiling by electric cords.

The chamber, which was about the size of Carlotta's living room, smelled like a garbage dump. Giuseppe attributed the musty odor to a partially-plugged ventilation shaft. There were no shelves; however, six large rectangular wooden tables were loaded with boxes. They were stacked so high he was afraid if he moved one of them they would all fall to the floor.

Giuseppe decided this is where he would spend the majority of his time. He would let his assistants handle the Secret Archives. Needless to say, it would take months to sort through all the boxes, but he had to start somewhere. He opened a box and removed the top document. Dated 1162, it was a decree from Pope Innocent the VIII. The pronouncement stated that anyone who dabbled in witchcraft or magic would be punished severely. Then he opened a letter written by Pope Gregory the IV. The date was 1229. The handwriting was faded and barely legible, but he could still read the decree. The pope assigned the duty of questioning suspected heretics to men who were far removed from the clergy. This allowed the inquisitors to act in the name of the pope and with his full authority. Giuseppe knew the decree was a way for the Church to distance itself and the Holy See from the many cruel acts the inquisitors performed. In those days, in order to gain confessions from heretics, the interrogators would often nail people to wooden planks and let them slowly bleed to death. He dug further and found that most letters in the box pertained to the Holy See and the Papal States, which at that time comprised most of Italy.

Giuseppe became so absorbed in what he was doing that he lost all track of time. He imagined what it would have been like to live in the seventeenth century and witness first hand the crimes that had taken place against humanity during the Catholic Inquisition.

One letter, which had been written by Pope Celestine the IV, authorized the Holy See to turn over heretics to secular authorities for execution, many of whom were burned alive. Another item of correspondence was from a pope to a cardinal stating he would sanction the spilling of blood provided it was based on justice and not hate. Then there was an edict from the Prefect of the Secretary of State indicating that the Roman Curia had granted civil authorities in the Papal States with the power of life and death. Another file contained five hundred sixteen execution orders, written between 1643 and 1762. All had been sanctioned by the Church.

Giuseppe found evidence that only in extreme cases would the Church attach the canonical penalty of excommunication to a clergyman for the crime of murder, which to a priest is equivalent to a death sentence. Some of the correspondence described homosexual acts committed by members of the clergy. One document dealt with the transfer of an archbishop for lewd conduct. The letter described how he had exposed himself in the rectory to several choirboys. Even a cardinal who held an important administrative post in the Vatican had been sanctioned for carousing with women of ill repute. Deeds that normally would have been punishable by torture, imprisonment, or both, were almost always forgiven by the apostolic penitentiary and the offender would either be transferred to another parish, demoted or both.

That he was now privy to the Church's darkest secrets weighed heavily on Giuseppe. It was difficult for him to return daily to read about the homosexual and heterosexual sex scandals. It was not as if he hadn't heard of their existence, but when he read about priests who violated canonical laws from handwritten documents, they had somehow become personal.

* * *

Giuseppe was pleased with the progress he was making. He had only started work in the Room of Dark Secrets three weeks ago and already he had gone through one of the boxes. He was a third of the way through the second box when he discovered a letter of gratitude written by a pope thanking Countess Ribaldi for making a substantial donation to the Vatican Library, which among other things was a rare grimoire titled *The Testament of Solomon*. Wasn't this the very book that Cardinal Romanus had asked him to look for? The name Ribaldi also sounded familiar, and then he remembered that his sister, Carlotta, had introduced him to a count with the same last name. Could the person who had received the letter of gratitude been a distant relative?

Intrigued, Giuseppe asked himself why an innocuous letter of gratitude, even one written by a pope to a countess, was stored among correspondence that revealed the darkest secrets of the Church. Could the Church have wanted to protect its wealthy patrons from blackmail? Could the Roman Curia have granted special favors to the Ribaldi family and didn't want that to be publicly known? Or could it be something about the grimoire itself? The question would have to wait as tonight he would be attending a party that was being hosted on a private yacht. The yacht, he was told, was owned by a rich banker from Siena.

CHAPTER 16

Frank Santino knew disaster was staring him in the face. His agent had no luck in finding him a gig, and he had to audition with Stover and the principal owners of the casino in three weeks. If he wasn't offered a new contract, at the rate Dottie was spending his money, he'd be broke in a matter of months. He figured if he ran out of money, he'd have to leave Las Vegas. He wasn't the type to welch on the money he owed to the casinos, but he would have little choice. Without a good-paying job, the money he owed was a great deal more than he could ever repay. He figured eventually they'd track him down, and then what?

The thought of skipping town owing people money depressed him so much he avoided Dottie and the hangers-on who were constantly mooching from her. Frank was beginning to realize he had made two big mistakes. His first slip-up had been not to listen to his mentor. Ron Erickson had told him years ago that if he wanted to continue being a headliner, he needed to always be on the lookout for new routines. His second blunder had been to marry Dottie. In the beginning, he believed she really cared for him, but now he realized that the only thing important to her was his money. And he didn't think it would much matter to her whether the money was his or someone else's. Well, unless a miracle occurred, he'd be broke and Dottie would have to find herself some other sucker.

Frank was alone in the study, feeling sorry for himself, when the phone rang. He didn't bother to pick up because he figured the call was for Dottie. Relieved that the phone had finally stopped ringing, he went back to reminiscing about better days when he heard Dottie's shrill voice. "It's for you, Frank. Someone by the name of Laura Hollingsworth wants to talk to you."

His heart lurched at the mention of her name. Why would she be calling? When he picked up the receiver, her voice sounded hysterical.

"Please slow down. I can't understand a word you are saying. Tell me what happened?"

"He is gone."

"Who is gone?"

"My dad. It's that accursed book. It ended up killing him!"

Frank was about to tell her that she wasn't being rational, but then thought better of it. "I'm so sorry. Is there anything I can do?"

"It's too late," she stammered. "I should have taken it away from him. I should have burned it!"

"No. For heaven's sake, don't do that. The book may hold the answer to your father's death."

"I'm telling you, it's cursed. I want it out of my—"

Frank was quick to interrupt. "I'll take it off your hands. I'll buy it from you. I'll pay you whatever you ask."

"I won't take a penny for it. I just want it out of my house!"

Frank couldn't believe what he was hearing. The miracle he had been praying for had just occurred. He knew he had to act quickly. Once Hollingsworth's attorneys found out about the grimoire, they'd talk the daughter of one of the wealthiest men in Los Angeles in letting some auction house sell it. "Miss Hollingsworth, I mean, Laura. Are you still on the line?"

"Yes. I'm here."

"You may be right. Maybe the book did cause your father's death. If I were you, I wouldn't touch it! Don't let anyone touch it. I am going to send my brother-in-law over to your house. He is a university professor," Frank lied. "His name is Max Hunter. I repeat, his name is Max Hunter. He will be flying in from San Francisco. All you have to do is tell him where it is. He will know what to do."

"All right. He can have it. I just want it gone."

Frank's heart was beating so fast that he rummaged through the medical cabinet, found a bottle of Dottie's tranquilizers, and washed a couple of them down with some water. Then he went to the liquor cabinet and poured himself a stiff shot of scotch. Not exactly the best combination his doctor would say, but he needed to stay calm. He should go and pick up the grimoire himself, but he had a show to do. He felt a twinge of guilt about playing on Laura Hollingsworth's fears, but he needed that book desperately. It was his only chance, and it had fallen so easily into his lap. He couldn't afford to blow this opportunity.

With trembling fingers, he punched in Max's number. After the third ring, he heard the tinny voice of an answering machine. He left a message and then decided to call him on his cell phone.

"This is Max."

"Where the hell are you?"

"I'm at a coffee shop. It's nice to get away from that roach-infested place where I live. What's up?"

"You need to fly to Los Angeles."

"What for?"

"Do you have your laptop with you?"

"Yes."

"Book a flight for today."

"And how do you expect me to pay for it?"

"Use the credit card Dottie gave you."

"What's the rush? I have an afternoon class so I can't go today. How about if I go tomorrow?"

"Damn it, Max. It has to be today! I need you to pick up *The Testament of Solomon*. Jesus, I can't believe my stroke of luck. I'll explain later, but you have to leave right away."

Frank's timing couldn't have been better. Max was going to call his brother-in-law to let him know he had spent the five-thousand-dollar retainer Frank had given him on books and tuition. He could still remember what Frank had told him the day he had agreed to write that request to the Vatican. "Help me out on this one, and I'll make sure you have enough money to finish school."

"Okay," Max said. "Give me the address and the name of the person I have to talk to."

CHAPTER 17

Giuseppe had accepted another invitation from his sister who had organized yet another fund-raiser, which was to be held at the Teatro dell'Opera di Roma. Some rather influential people in Italy had talked the famous singer, Andrea Boccelli, to perform songs from *La bohème*, which was Giuseppe's favorite opera. Although tickets for the one-night performance had been sold out, Carlotta had an extra one for him. She had also invited him to a small dinner party before the late evening performance.

Giuseppe was to be at the villa for cocktails at five o'clock, but no one in Italy ever came to a party on time so he had planned to arrive fashionably late at five-forty-five. The butler who let him in asked him to wait in the drawing room. Wait for what? And then he remembered there had been a time change. Instead of arriving forty-five minutes late, he was actually fifteen minutes early. To leave and then come back would have been awkward so he decided to walk the grounds. He was mulling over some ideas to propose to his staff at the archives when loud voices coming from a second-story window interrupted his thoughts.

"I will not put any of my money into that foolhardy investment," Carlotta yelled.

"There is nothing foolhardy about it," her husband Antonio countered. "Saunders is a very astute businessman. He has a million euros of his own money in this land deal." His voice grew shriller. "As you know, the hotel I'm building in Venice is costing me a great deal more than I thought."

"That's not my problem," Carlotta replied, her voice strident. "Besides, you know most of the money father left me is in a trust. I only get to spend the interest. Giuseppe is the trustee. Why don't you ask him?"

"I was hoping you would do that for me."

"Why should I? It's your project, not mine," Carlotta countered.

Giuseppe felt like an eavesdropper. It made him uncomfortable to be privy to such personal information. He walked away from the window and into the drawing room.

Within moments Carlotta came to greet him. He was amazed at her composure. He certainly couldn't have controlled his emotions had he been involved in such an argument.

"I know what you are about to say, but no apology is necessary," she said. "Regardless of what time it is, the door to this house is always open to you." When she walked up to him, he automatically extended his ring, but instead of kissing it, she kissed him on both cheeks. "You may be a cardinal, but I'm still your sister. How is the pope doing?"

"Not well, I'm afraid."

"I'm sorry to hear that. Something to drink?"

"Grappa if you have it."

She pulled a cord and a waiter appeared with a crystal decanter and two glasses.

"Leave the tray on the sideboard, Caprio. I'd like to pour. Is the staff ready for our guests?"

The servant bowed. "The arrangements have been finalized. Would you like to inspect the dining room?"

"No," Carlotta said. "I don't think that will be necessary." She turned toward Giuseppe, an impish grin on her face.

"What is it, sister? I know you are up to something. Come on. You'd better come clean."

"Well, all right. I was going to surprise you, but you know me. I'm not good at keeping secrets. I invited only two guests for dinner."

Giuseppe laughed. "Only two? They must be pretty important people," he mused.

"They are, or at least one is. I've been trying to get you to meet this person for six months. Finally, my perseverance has paid off. Tonight you, my dear brother, will be eating dinner with the richest man in all of Italy."

"Well, he can't be the richest man. I say this because the richest is Prime Minister Silvio Berlusconi."

At that moment Antonio entered the room. "I knew you wouldn't be able to keep it a surprise." He walked up to Giuseppe with a gleam in his eye. "I was just informed that the prime minister's limousine has arrived."

CHAPTER 18

Max Hunter was awestruck when he saw the size of Hollingsworth's estate. He thought Frank and Dottie lived in luxury, but their home was nothing compared to this. His only hope was that someday he would be able to afford a place the size of Hollingsworth's gatehouse.

The guard who approached him actually wore a uniform and had a side arm strapped to his belt.

"May I help you?"

Although he sounded courteous enough, Max could tell by the tone of his voice that this was one man who wouldn't put up with any nonsense.

"My name is Max Hunter. I was told to come by and pick up a book."

The guard glanced at a clipboard and then shook his head. "No one told me you were coming."

"I assure you I am not making it up. Miss Hollingsworth is expecting me."

"Just a moment." The guard picked up a phone, and a few minutes later one of the iron gates leading to the mansion swung open. Max took a deep breath and forged ahead. He pulled the rental car in front of the fountain with the dolphins. By the time he was close enough to the double doors with the stained-glass windows, one of them opened and a servant in a butler's uniform appeared. "Mister Max Hunter?" he asked.

Mister Max Hunter. No one had ever called him anything, but Max. "Yes. I'm Max Hunter."

"Come with me, please."

Max followed the butler past a grand staircase down a hallway where numerous old oil paintings covered the walls. Eventually he found himself standing in front of a set of wooden doors. The butler twisted a bronze knob, at least Max thought it was bronze, and found himself in a room completely surrounded by shelves, and every one of them was crammed full of books. Most were bound in leather and looked quite old.

The butler pointed to a book that lay on top of a large mahogany desk. Max assumed it was the grimoire. He thought it strange that the servant wouldn't look at it. "That's the book Miss Hollingsworth wants you to have. Please take it and leave."

Max placed the leather-bound manuscript in his tattered briefcase and followed the butler out of the room. He was at the airport waiting for the plane that would take him to Las Vegas when his cell phone buzzed. "Do you have it?"

"Yes. It's in my briefcase."

"Where's the briefcase?" Frank Santino asked.

"Where the hell do you think it is? I am holding it in one hand and the phone in the other."

Frank's tone softened. "Don't get testy. I just want to make sure you don't let it out of your sight."

"I know, Frank. You've only told me a hundred times."

"Call me once you arrive. If I'm tied up, I'll have Dottie pick you up."

"Okay. I take it I'm back on the payroll?"

"I'll pay you the per diem rate we agreed upon. I told you I would. You should know by now I wouldn't go back on my word."

"Okay, I just wanted to make sure we're on the same page. I'll get there as soon as I can."

"Max, I want you to promise me that you will not take that book out of your briefcase. Not even a peek. Understood?"

"Yeah, sure. I don't know why all this secrecy is necessary though. I mean, it may be old and rare, but it's only a book."

"Not to me, it isn't. That grimoire is going to make me the most famous magician in the world!"

CHAPTER 19

Giuseppe woke up in a good mood. He had gotten along fabulously with Prime Minister Berlusconi and his charming wife. In fact so splendidly that Mrs. Berlusconi had extended an invitation for him to attend a party at her villa in Assisi. It seemed she also wanted to help him become the next bishop of Rome.

After Mass, Giuseppe had a hearty breakfast in the smaller of three dining rooms reserved for cardinals. Then he entered the Room of Dark Secrets where he planned to spend the day.

It was almost lunchtime when he came upon an undated communiqué written to a pope which piqued his interest. Although it was unsigned, it did contain a Vatican Library seal. The memo simply stated that because of an archbishop's carelessness, a rare book on mysticism was missing. Apparently, instead of returning the manuscript to its designated place, the archbishop had left it on top of one of the tables that scholars normally used when conducting research. Neither the archbishop's name nor the title of the book was mentioned, but that particular item of correspondence did state that if the pope wanted further information, a full accounting of the incident would be provided to His Holiness.

Giuseppe read the letter again. The book the letter was referring to had to be *The Testament of Solomon*. After all, how many grimoires could go missing from the Vatican Library?

Another day passed before Giuseppe found yet another file. This one provided a full accounting of the events that must have transpired after the pope had been briefed on the grimoire's theft. But this memorandum had a name attached to it. Pope Alexander the VII had reprimanded Archbishop Alberto Dominique for his carelessness and informed him there would be dire consequences if he didn't find the person who had stolen *The Testament of Solomon*.

Giuseppe read the memorandum again. Archbishop Alberto Dominique. Why did the name sound familiar? Then he remembered that the archbishop was the same one who had received a letter of gratitude from Cardinal Cervini for recovering *The Testament of Solomon*. He still remembered the name because a few weeks ago he had made a copy of the letter of gratitude Cardinal Romanus had given him.

Giuseppe read the memorandum a third time and mentally reviewed what he knew so far.

Fact one: *The Testament of Solomon* had been donated to the Vatican Library by Countess Ribaldi. Fact two: Pope Alexander the VII criticized Archbishop Alberto Dominique for his carelessness in the handling of the grimoire. Fact three: A letter of gratitude had been written to the same Archbishop by Cardinal Cervini for finding the grimoire and returning it to the Vatican Library.

There had to be more to this story. Much more. Something else must have transpired, something more than just a missing grimoire. It was obviously not in the Vatican Library, and because there was no record of the book being transferred to the Secret Archives, he figured it had to be somewhere here in the Room of Dark Secrets.

Giuseppe believed something sinister must have happened or else why would the Church want all correspondence that pertained to the grimoire kept secret? Determined to get to the bottom of the mysterious disappearance of the grimoire, he kept searching. He read every document in the box where he had found the initial letter, but found no further communication regarding *The Testament of Solomon*. He was certain there was other correspondence. There had to be, but the letters had obviously been placed in some of the other boxes. Was this done because someone had tried to make the letters more difficult to find? Or was this just another example of sloppy record-keeping? Exactly what had transpired in the seventeenth century that had to be kept under lock and key in this very special secret room, and where was the grimoire itself?

Tired and hungry, Giuseppe turned off the lights, locked the massive door and headed back up the tunnel to the Secret Archives. He checked his computer for emails, went to evening Mass, and then headed toward his apartment.

The Swiss sentries who stood guard over the east wing of the apartments that housed some twenty cardinals instantly recognized Giuseppe and let him pass. Although the apartments had been recently remodeled, the age-old tradition of not having locks on individual living quarters was still very much in place. After all, next to the pope, cardinals were the highest-ranking clerics in the Vatican. If cardinals couldn't be trusted, then whom could one trust?

Giuseppe had been asleep for less than an hour, when the cell phone he kept near his bed jarred him awake. He glanced at his watch and wondered who could be calling him at eleven o'clock at night.

Although he recognized Carlotta's voice, he couldn't understand what she was saying because she sounded panic-stricken. "Calm down, Carlotta. Please calm down. Start from the beginning and talk slower."

"It's Antonio, Giuseppe. We just had the biggest fight. He told me I was selfish and said that unless I loaned him the money he needed he'd be ruined."

Giuseppe recalled the earlier argument between Carlotta and Antonio, but he did not want Carlotta to know he had heard them bickering. "Why does he want you to lend him money? Antonio is rich. He owns several hotels, doesn't he?"

"Yes", Carlotta sobbed. "But the fool has mortgaged all of them to the hilt. Do you remember having dinner with an investor by the name of Saunders?" Carlotta didn't wait for Giuseppe to answer. "Antonio has sunk several million euros into a real estate venture in Acapulco, Mexico. I think it's called Punta Dora. Saunders told Antonio he would lose his entire investment if he didn't come up with more money."

Giuseppe sighed; even the rich could go broke. "How much more?"

"He wants one and a half million euros. That's why I am calling you. I can't lend him that kind of money without your permission."

Although technically Giuseppe owned half of the family's trust, he always donated his share of the interest earned from the trust's investments to the Church.

"One and a half million is a lot of money." He thought for a moment before continuing. "I would agree to the loan on one condition. I want to check out this Saunders and particularly the Punta Dora project. What's his first name?

"I believe it's Justin. Yes, I'm sure. Justin Saunders."

"Tell Antonio you have talked with me and that I shall give him my answer within the week. If the real estate venture is basically sound, I'll agree to the loan. However, if I determine he'd be throwing your good money away, I won't let him have a penny."

Carlotta's relief was almost palpable. "Oh, Giuseppe, I knew I could count on you to help me with this matter. Thank you so much."

"You are welcome, my dear sister, but now would you please let me go back to sleep?"

But sleep did not come easily. Giuseppe did not appreciate Antonio's roughshod tactics. Instead of trying to coerce Carlotta in loaning him the money, Antonio should have had this conversation with him. His brother-in-law knew perfectly well he was the trustee of the estate and it would be up to him and not Carlotta to lend him the money.

Giuseppe thought back to when Antonio had purchased the villa for Carlotta, an extravagant gift to say the least. Although Giuseppe had always known Antonio made snap decisions, even when millions of euros were at stake, he had always believed him to use good judgment—until now, that is.

CHAPTER 20

Max still had an hour or so before his flight so he bought a newspaper, placed the briefcase that contained the grimoire on his lap, and proceeded to read the sports page. Once he realized he was just looking at the words, he put the paper aside. All he could think of was the grimoire. Did *The Testament of Solomon* really contain the secrets of the ancients, or was this just another book on the occult that made false promises to its readers? It was right there on his lap. Although Frank had told him not to look at it, he couldn't see the harm. Besides, Frank would never know.

Max unbuckled the two clasps of his tattered briefcase, and glanced around to make sure no one was paying him any attention. He removed the grimoire and placed it on his lap. The first thing he noticed was the book was quite heavy. It took a few minutes for him to leaf through the pages, all three hundred sixteen of them. The cover had no title and was made from the skin of some animal. The fringes of the book were slightly charred and so were a few of the pages, but all in all, considering its age, the grimoire seemed to be in pretty good shape.

He had been told the grimoire had been written in Italian so he assumed it would be easy to read, but he was mistaken. The scribe's penmanship wasn't the problem. Although he could pronounce most of the words, he had trouble recognizing a number of them. Fortunately, the vernacular was in Sicilian, a dialect Max was familiar with. Because a number of words were Latinized, he knew he would need to avail himself of a Latin-to-Italian dictionary. He carefully replaced the book inside the briefcase and proceeded to board his flight.

Once he was settled in his seat, he took another look at the grimoire. It was divided into three main sections. The first dealt with a series of chants that were supposed to summon spirits. Whether they were good or evil, he did not know. The second part of the book dealt with paranormal activities that if used properly, trained the mind to defy gravity. This, he knew, was the section Frank would want to concentrate on. The last segment was what interested him the most. It showed how one's mind could travel to a place where the knowledge of the universe was stored.

Max's hands were shaking. He felt as if a hundred ants were crawling up and down his back. Nerves, he supposed. He knew that in helping Frank, he would have ample opportunities to study the book. It was conceivable that the grimoire would allow him to reach certain conclusions as to the existence or nonexistence of the akashic records. If nothing else, the manuscript would definitely help him complete his doctoral dissertation.

In a way, Max's welfare was just as dependent on the grimoire as Frank's was. He was tired of having to rely on his sister's handouts and Frank's generosity. He hoped the book would help him secure his own future to the point where he could become his own person. He desperately wanted to move out of that rathole one-room apartment of his so he could rent a small, clean place of his own.

CHAPTER 21

Giuseppe, unlike many of his generation, excelled at maneuvering through hyperspace. He researched Justin Saunders and the Punta Dora project, and what he found, he did not like. It didn't take him long to discover that one of Saunders's companies owned the strip of land where the Punta Dora Hotel was to be built; however, the interesting part was Saunders didn't have any of his own money invested in the project itself. This bothered Giuseppe a great deal. Why was Saunders limiting his involvement? Is there any other way he could benefit from the project's collapse? Of course! If Saunders's investors failed to put in enough money to finish the project, the land company Saunders owned could take over, and people like Antonio, who had paid for the permits, land surveys and geological reports would receive nothing for their money.

His heart went out to Carlotta and her family. But there was no way he was going to sanction the withdrawal of funds from the trust, no way was he going to throw good money after bad. His first inclination had been to call Antonio to let him know what he had discovered. But then he thought better of it. He'd seen Antonio get extremely agitated at times. Giuseppe was afraid if he were to relate such sensitive information over the phone, Antonio's emotions might cloud his judgment. So he sent him an email instead. He suggested Antonio hire a real estate attorney before placing any additional money in the project.

Giuseppe possessed the uncanny ability to focus on a particular task until he completed it. Now that he had made his recommendations to Antonio, he put the matter behind him. He was now eager to get back to the Room of Dark Secrets. After rummaging through yet another box, Giuseppe hit the proverbial jackpot. There were four letters in a file that had been wedged between two stacks of papal documents. If he had not examined every item in the box, he definitely would have missed the folder.

The more he read, the more he became certain that all four letters pertained to *The Testament of Solomon.*

The first was a letter to Pope Alexander VII, written by a Cardinal Saffrino. In it Saffrino stated that two priests from the Santa Passera Parish had witnessed Archbishop Alberto Dominique struggle over a book with a local priest by the name of Father Simon Anglacio. Once the archbishop had possession of the book, they were horrified to see Dominique push Father Anglacio into a raging fire.

The second item of correspondence carried the papal seal. It was from Pope Alexander VII addressed to the Prefect of the Vatican Library, Cardinal Cervini. The pope stated an urgent matter had been brought to his attention by Cardinal Saffrino, who at the time was in charge of judiciary matters for the Holy See. The pope requested that Cervini not only reverify the story the two witnesses had related to Saffrino, but also question the alleged perpetrator, Archbishop Alberto Dominique.

A terse memo from Cardinal Cervini to the pope dated several days later simply stated that when questioned, Archbishop Alberto Dominique did not deny a struggle had occurred and that Father Anglacio did, in fact, end up in the fire.

The last letter Giuseppe had come across was from Cardinal Saffrino to Pope Alexander VII dated several weeks later. Saffrino suggested the matter be turned over for prosecution to the Vatican High Court because the priests who had witnessed the altercation between the two clergymen had apparently informed the parishioners of the crime. Furious that a cleric from their church was murdered by a Vatican archbishop, the parishioners came en masse to the Vatican demanding that justice be served.

Giuseppe still didn't have the whole story, but he was definitely intrigued. He wondered what position the High Court would have taken regarding Archbishop Dominique? Did they find him innocent or guilty? Usually, clerics who had been found guilty of lesser crimes were exonerated by the Ecumenical Penitentiary, whose business was to show mercy. The Prefect of the Ecumenical Penitentiary routinely pardoned clergyman for lesser sins. Giuseppe had run across hundreds of files where priests had been forgiven for breaking canonical vows such as conducting a Black Mass or taking it upon themselves to perform exorcisms which had not been sanctioned by the Church. Those kinds of offenses were common, particularly in the seventeenth and eighteenth centuries. But one priest murdering another? This was no ordinary crime. A crime that certainly could not have been forgiven.

Although these events had taken place centuries ago, Giuseppe was determined to find out how this had all played out. Not so much because he was curious as to what had taken place, even though he was, but because of the recent outcry and public outrage over cover-ups by the Church involving pedophile priests. The image of his beloved Church was already tarnished. He certainly hoped, even prayed, that the Vatican High Court had metered out a just punishment for Archbishop Alberto Dominique.

CHAPTER 22

Frank Santino now wished he hadn't agreed to perform a special matinee on this particular Saturday. He was tired, and he still had another show to do before he could think of the grimoire. He mustered all of his resolve and walked out on the stage to a resounding round of applause. Although most of the holographic images he produced had been recorded in advance, he still had to time the transmission of a number of lasers in order to recreate the illusions.

What the audience did not know and would never find out was that attached to each of Frank's fingers was a flesh-colored mechanical device no larger than the stub of a pencil. When activated, Frank could scatter numerous laser beams of light onto the stage. It had taken him several years to perfect the technique of dispersing laser beams from pre-recorded images so he could later reconstruct the icons at will. The three-dimensional illusions he reproduced looked so authentic that many in the audience believed the demons and devils they were seeing were actually real.

As soon as the show ended, he took his bows and headed for his dressing room where he was surprised to find Richard Stover. He was sitting in his only chair, chewing on one of his obscenely fat cigars. Stover took it out of his mouth just long enough to say, "Great act, Frank, great act. I've got to give it to you. The audience always swallows all of your illusionary bullshit."

Frank was in no mood for Stover's condescending attitude. "What are you doing here?"

Much like a turtle, Stover reared his head from a token neck. "I thought I'd drop in to se how you were doing with the new act." A lopsided grin appeared on his pugnacious face. "I'm disappointed. I thought by now you would have come up with some changes to your routine."

Not only was Frank tired, but he was anxious to get home so he could take a look at the grimoire. Besides, he felt he had put up with Stover's verbal abuse long enough. Let him get pissed off, but Stover had opened the door and Frank wasn't about to let his remark fly.

"What is it you want me to do? I thought you wanted me to come up with an entirely new show and not revamp the old one. I wish you'd make up your mind. Or have you decided to renege on your promise?"

Stover's jaw tightened. The look he gave Frank clearly indicated that Frank had crossed the line. Then Stover relaxed and placed one of his pudgy hands on Frank's shoulder. "No, no. You do need to come up with a new act. I just thought you might have put something together by now."

Frank gritted his teeth. "I'm still working on it."

"Sure, sure." Stover walked toward the door, took the cigar out of his mouth, and as an afterthought said, "I hope I won't be disappointed. It wouldn't bode well for you if the owners of the Boulevardier thought your new routine couldn't cut it."

Frank wanted to shout after him—my ass is not the only one on the line—but he knew he was already treading on thin ice based on his earlier comment so he kept his mouth shut. On his way out, he ran into Pete, the stagehand. "Why in hell did you allow Stover in my dressing room?"

"Well, Frank, being that he is . . ."

"I don't care if he's President of the United States. This is my dressing room. The next time you pull a stunt like that, you'll be pounding the pavement looking for a job."

By the time, Frank pulled the Ferrari into his garage, his anger was replaced with anticipation. Dottie had called earlier to tell him she had picked Max up from the airport. He knew if Max was waiting for him, then so was the grimoire!

The minute Frank set foot in the house, he found Max and led him to the den. "You do have it, don't you?"

"Of course I do."

"Have you read any of it? Don't lie to me. Tell me the truth."

"I took a quick look."

"And what do you make of it?"

Max removed the grimoire from his briefcase and handed it to Frank. "I'm not sure. The good news is that most of it is written in Italian; however, the language has changed over the last thousand years. The vernacular is Sicilian, so I can read most of the words, but . . ."

"But what? If you can read most of the words, then what's the problem?"

Max sighed. "Many words are in Latin. The irony here is that many more people can read Latin than Sicilian, but I'm not one of them." Max gave Frank a sheepish look. "I'm ashamed to say I never bothered to study Latin in school."

A look of exasperation appeared on Frank's face. "So what you are saying is that you can't read the grimoire."

"No. I'm not saying that at all. I can read the words. I think I'll even be able to pronounce them correctly. You will most likely be able to read from the grimoire as well. The reason I'm being hesitant is that I'm not sure I'll be able to accurately interpret the passages. Connotations change, particularly over a long span of time, but I'll work it out. That's why we have dictionaries."

Another stumbling block Frank did not need. "I hope so. I sure as heck don't want a stranger looking at the book." Frank appeared to be satisfied with Max's answer. "Okay, so what do you think?"

Max appeared to give Frank's question some thought. "From what I can gather, *The Testament of Solomon* is an extremely different type of book. I could be wrong, but I believe if you were to chant the incantations in a certain way, you might attain your objective."

"Which is?"

"You are still testing me, aren't you, Frank?"

"No. I'm not. You are the expert here."

"Although I've read a lot about the akashic records, I'm not an expert. It's a very difficult concept to grasp, harder still to put into words. But I think what has to happen is you must figure out a way to cross over the threshold of consciousness to a power that's behind the throne of thought."

Frank glanced at the grimoire. "And just how do I go about doing that?"

"I don't know. My guess is you are going to have to work with the book, experiment, try different things. All I can tell you is that the human mind works in strange ways. What may work for me may not work for you."

Frank pushed the grimoire aside. "I'm not interested in learning about ancient knowledge, Max. All I want to do is be able to levitate and maybe move some objects around a stage."

Max walked over to where Frank was sitting. "If you look at the book, you'll see there are three major sections to it. To my way of thinking, it doesn't make much difference whether you attempt to conjure demons, levitate, or enter the storehouse of knowledge that some call the akashic records. You will get to where you want to go through hypnosis."

"You mean a trancelike state?"

"Yes. While majoring in philosophy, I took a three-unit course dealing with trances. There are basically two types. If you were to enter a hypnotic trance, you would have control of your mental faculties."

"Is that why a hypnotist can't make you do things you wouldn't do normally?"

"See, Frank? You know more than you think you do. But in order to accomplish your objective, you must enter a possessory trance."

"And what exactly is that?"

"Mind you, all I can do is speak theoretically. I've never known anyone who has actually experienced this kind of trance; from my limited knowledge few people have. However, there are books on the subject, and I've probably read most of them."

Frank didn't want to have a philosophical discussion about trances. All he wanted to know was whether the book could help him come up with some different routines. "Okay, so can you describe what will happen if I could enter this so-called possessory trance?"

"You could get hurt, even die. I say this because if you end up using the book to place yourself into this trance, you will no longer be you. You would be at the mercy of whatever it is your mind would have conjured."

"Jesus, Max. You aren't making any sense."

"Okay, then let me put it to you this way. In order for you to succeed, you will have to learn how to block all extraneous thoughts from your mind. Think of the mind as a maze of compartments. You must learn to vacate all of them, clear the mind of all thoughts but one, and in your case that would be levitation." Max paused to gather his thoughts. "Another way of putting it is, you wouldn't want any ideas to enter your mind that weren't somehow connected to levitation. If you can manage to do this, your mind will become extremely powerful. Think of your mind as a filter. If you learn how to control what goes through the filter, you'll master the concept of mind control. What I'm talking about here, Frank, is pure energy of thought."

"My God. Do you realize what you are saying? You are talking about something . . . something that's supernatural."

Max slid the grimoire closer to Frank. "They accused Galileo of sorcery or have you forgotten? For some reason all of us, me included, categorize things as supernatural or paranormal if we don't understand them. Supernatural? Maybe, maybe not, but one thing I know for sure. If you can learn to master the grimoire, you'll end up with one hell of a show!"

CHAPTER 23

Cardinal Giuseppe Mercati knew canon law mandated that all records pertaining to priests' misbehaviors be kept either in the Secret Archives or in the Room of Dark Secrets. Needless to say, when he discovered that Archbishop Dominique had pushed Father Anglacio into a fire, he figured the Room of Dark Secrets should contain the trial records of such an important case.

Giuseppe had methodically gone through all the boxes that had been stacked on the first table. Now that he was searching for something specific, he didn't bother to scrutinize every piece of correspondence in a file. He finally found what he was looking for in a box on the third table. The Vatican High Court rarely dealt with capital offenses, but the murder of a parish priest was such a heinous crime that a special tribunal of judges had been appointed by Pope Alexander the VII to hear the case. The judicial branch of the Holy See had provided a prosecutor as well as a trial lawyer to represent the accused. Fortunately, all accounts of the one-day trial were recorded by a scribe. There wasn't all that much information in the file so it didn't take Giuseppe long to read it.

The court first listened to the two priests who had witnessed the dastardly deed. They described in detail what they had seen. Both priests swore they heard Archbishop Dominique and Father Anglacio argue over the grimoire. The archbishop insisted that Father Anglacio had no right to destroy it. Then, when Father Anglacio had thrown the book into the burning embers, Dominique had pushed Anglacio into the fire and rescued the grimoire. One of the two priests also told the tribunal that he recognized Archbishop Dominique as he had seen him at the parish on more than one occasion and although it was a moonless night, Dominique's face was clearly visible as he was standing quite close to the blazing fire.

Archbishop Dominique called no witnesses, but he did testify in his own defense. Dominique claimed Father Anglacio had lost his footing when they had struggled over the grimoire. Despite of what the two witnesses had said, Dominique insisted the fall had been purely accidental. Dominique recognized the court might wonder why he hadn't come to Anglacio's assistance and had pulled the grimoire out of the fire instead. Why did he save the book? He told the tribunal he had asked himself the question many times. His only justification was that Pope Alexander the VII had charged him with the responsibility of finding the book as it had been stolen from the Vatican Library. He stressed that everything had happened so quickly. Perhaps, in a moment of panic, he had subconsciously felt he couldn't ignore an order from the Holy Father, regardless of the consequences. For this reason, he had also put himself at personal risk by placing his hand in the fire to retrieve the grimoire. He sincerely regretted Father Anglacio's death and prayed daily for the salvation of his soul.

The next to the last page in the file wasn't really a page, it was a terse memo written anonymously to the Vatican High Court. The cursive writing was faded and difficult to read, but Giuseppe finally managed to make it out. It said:

> The crowd outside the Vatican's walls is now an angry mob. They want justice. They want blood. If you let the archbishop live, many could die.

Then he found an official looking document. It was addressed to the Roman Curia. The seal clearly indicated it was from the High Court:

> The tribunal has determined that in his eagerness to return *The Testament of Solomon* to its rightful place, Archbishop Dominique had used extremely poor judgment and the violent act he committed upon a member of the clergy was not only incomprehensible, but also inexcusable.

The next paragraph sent a cold chill down Giuseppe's spine:

Archbishop Dominique, the Vatican High Court finds you guilty of the high crime of murder. You are to be taken herewith from this court under guard to a place where you shall be detained. From there you will be taken to the gallows where you shall be hanged by the neck until you are dead.

Giuseppe was a scholar; therefore, he was quite familiar with Vatican history. Although the Holy See had sanctioned numerous executions in the Papal States, none had been carried out within the Vatican itself, and to his knowledge no priest had suffered the ultimate penalty of death. If, in fact, Archbishop Dominique had been hanged, then there had to be a record of the execution.

Giuseppe renewed his search. He had to find out what happened. He was more determined than ever to get at the truth.

CHAPTER 24

Frank didn't harbor any illusions and, unlike Max, acknowledged that he had never been a soul-searching type of person. Although not stupid, he wasn't a deep thinker. He thought of himself as a man of action, not a man of reflection. He would need assistance if he was ever going to internalize the grimoire, help that Max wasn't in a position to provide.

Dottie was always bragging about her yoga instructor and how the meditation she did with him helped her through her day. What the hell? Frank was desperate. This would at least be a start.

He arranged private sessions with the yogi and would sit cross-legged with him on a mat and practice breathing exercises. Five breaths in, five breaths out. He couldn't for the life of him figure out what these exercises had to do with clearing his mind of extraneous thoughts, but he decided it would be best not to question the yogi.

Next, he was told he needed to create an image of a yellow pencil in his mind, not only the wooden portion of the pencil, but also the eraser and the gold metal band that held the eraser in place. He focused on that image, and only on that image, for five minutes at a time, then ten, then twenty, and still the yogi wasn't satisfied. After a week of staring at the pencil, Frank could go an hour before losing his concentration. Of course, the minute that happened, extraneous thoughts would immediately enter his mind.

Frank met with the yogi daily for two weeks before he began to read passages from the grimoire. But the words seemed totally meaningless. Time and time again, he would sound them out, and for what purpose? The book certainly wasn't bringing him any closer to his goal, and he was fast running out of time. Frank remembered that Max had told him as long as he was conscious of what he was doing, and was aware of his surroundings, it meant he wasn't in a trance. His frustration grew with each passing day. He had convinced himself *The Testament of Solomon* was a grimoire that consisted of empty words, but he continued to read from it. Sometimes he would chant the words. At other times, he would just recite them, but nothing seemed to work. He doubled the amount of time he had been spending with his yoga instructor. Frank was not a patient man, but he knew the book was his only hope.

Although he had redoubled his efforts to master the grimoire, he was nowhere near where Laura Hollingsworth had said her father was. Frank recalled Laura telling him how he had aged once he had become obsessed with the book. She had also told him that once her father had been with the grimoire for a while, she had found it impossible to take it away from him.

At the moment, Frank felt exactly the opposite about the book. He loathed to pick it up and had to force himself to read the passages. And he certainly didn't think he would ever get to the point where he would become fixated with it.

The day of reckoning was drawing near. Richard Stover had called to tell him that the owners of the Boulevardier expected him to audition no later than two weeks from Tuesday. That meant he only had fourteen days to come up with something.

Frank decided to take the grimoire to a place where he could be alone with the book. There were too many distractions at the house. If it wasn't Dottie who either wanted or needed something, it was Max who would be hovering nearby dispensing advice. He ended up renting a room at the Boulevardier. The amphitheater was within walking distance and when he was not performing, he could spend his free time undisturbed with the book. Dottie complained, but the hell with her. He felt he had to take these drastic measures or else he'd end up losing his job for sure.

At two o'clock one morning Frank was lying in bed chanting words from the grimoire when suddenly the lights flicked off. With the drapes closed, it was pitch black in the room. He remembered he had a Zippo lighter in his pants pocket. Although he had quit smoking cigarettes, he carried it around with him because there were occasions when he would light up a joint. He groped around in the dark, and finally managed to find it.

The bright flame of the lighter cast an eerie glow over the grimoire. He opened the book and began to recite a few phrases. After he had read a page or so, he could no longer see the words. But it didn't really matter. One moment there had been nothing but an empty black void. Then a thousand points of light seemed to leap out of his head much like an exploding rocket on the Fourth of July.

He wasn't consciously aware of the force entering his very being. The energy had come as an infiltrator would have arrived, without any warning. Although he had not tested its presence, subconsciously he knew it was there. He had fought it, tried to keep it from tunneling into his system, but the defense only lasted for a couple seconds. It unleashed a fear so intense he thought he was going to scream; however, no sound came from his mouth. Frank attempted to objectify the agony he was feeling. He tried to examine the mental reality of what was happening as if he were a product of another mind, a scientific phenomenon to be studied.

That worked for a bit, but then that defense, too, became overwhelmed by the force.

Force . . . That was it! In a conscious sense, that was the word he had been groping for. It was a force, not an entity, not a presence—but a force. He felt his body tense as if it, too, was trying to fight the entry of all of that energy. At that very moment his mind spasmed, just as his body did, and he lost control of all conscious thought.

As if by some preset signal, his eyeballs rolled upward and his lids began to twitch. At first he was sure his head would explode, but the pain only lasted for an instant. For the first time in his life, Frank Santino experienced the feeling of power, real power. Now he knew. Now he understood. The force had been knocking on the door of his soul. His body had reacted to the force, much like it would have, had a virus tried to poison his blood. His defense mechanism had automatically kicked in. It was only when he had relaxed that his body had succumbed and allowed the force to enter his mind.

Just then the lights came back on, and somehow he had managed to rip himself free from its vicelike grasp. One minute it was there, a power so intense he felt he could rearrange the position of the stars, and the next all he could feel was the cold sweat streaming in rivulets down his face.

That was when Frank realized he had to make a choice. He could sell the book so as not to be tempted to pick it up again or he could continue to read from it. He instinctively knew if he ever recited those phrases again, he would become a prisoner of the book. Like a heroin addict craving a fix, he would never be able to part with the grimoire.

He sat for the longest time and stared at the book's untitled cover.

Then, ever so slowly, he again recited the ancient words from the mystical text, a text he now knew would soon give him the ability to do things no human would ever be able accomplish—at least not without the grimoire.

CHAPTER 25

Frank felt as if someone else's legs were propelling him toward the bank of elevators. He entered the casino and approached one of the crap tables. "Is my line of credit still good?" he asked the pit boss.

"Of course, Mr. Santino. How much would you like?"

"Give me twenty thousand." Even though the voice was his, it was as if someone else had mouthed the words. His bets were modest until it was his turn to roll the dice. Frank placed twenty black chips on the pass line. Two thousand dollars was certainly a large bet, but the Boulevardier's maximum limit was twice that amount. He didn't actually will a four and a three to come up. At least he didn't consciously think he had. When the dice left his hands, he pictured an image of four dots on one cube and three dots on the other. When he looked up, he was staring at a seven. He looked twice just to make certain he hadn't made a mistake. Frank let the full amount ride. This time he pictured a six. Why not? After all, wasn't that his favorite number? Actually, the image he had formed in his mind had been quite specific. He hadn't visualized a five and a one or a four and a two. Instead, he had fashioned an image of two threes.

He knew even before the dice rolled to a stop that what he had formed in his mind would become a reality. When Frank rolled a four, he had the croupier place several thousand dollars worth of chips on the field numbers. The five, eight, nine, and ten gave good odds, so why not take maximum advantage of his newly found talent? He pictured the cubes rolling to a stop on the felt-lined table; a two and a three, a four and another four, a four and a five and finally a pair of fives. Within several minutes, he upgraded his large stack of five-hundred-dollar chips to a smaller stack of thousand-dollar chips. He knew he could keep winning for hours at a stretch, but he didn't want the casino to get suspicious so he purposely pulled his large stack of chips off the field numbers and crapped out.

Frank held the dice just long enough not to arouse suspicion. Forty-five minutes was a phenomenal streak of luck some would say, but certainly not an impossible accomplishment. Of course in Frank's case, luck had nothing to do with it. After deducting what Frank had borrowed from the table, the croupier placed Frank's winnings in front of him. The stack of chips was so large that the pit boss handed him a couple of trays so he could take them to the teller's cage. Frank flipped one of the croupiers a couple of black chips. "You made me a winner for a change, Charlie."

The croupier acknowledged Frank's tip by tapping the chips on the felt-lined table. "Thank you, Mr. Santino. Come back soon."

"You bet I will." Frank had to work at keeping a straight face. "I have a feeling my luck might hold out a while longer."

A security guard followed Frank to the cashier's cage. Frank waited patiently for the girl to count the multitude of chips. There were so many that she ended up counting them three times.

"How much do I have?" Frank asked.

"Ninety-six thousand, Mr. Santino. How do you want it?"

"First, I need you to tell me what I owe."

The cashier turned to her computer. "Thirty-six five." She announced that fact as if the money she was talking about was a mere pittance.

"Clear my tab, and I'll take an IOU for the rest. The casino can write me a check. I'll pick it up later."

Once he was back in his room, he willed himself out of the trance. His head hurt like hell. He felt as if his brain was a sponge and someone had just wrung it dry. He took several Vicodin tablets for the pain and placed a damp washcloth on top of his forehead. He lay down hoping it wouldn't take long for the Vicodin to kick in, but an hour later the searing pain was still there, just beneath his skull. It felt that whatever had possessed his mind had violated his very being.

He tried to reach the phone. The nightstand was no more than a foot away, but he didn't have the strength to pick up the receiver. Scared and alone, he finally drifted off into a fitful sleep.

He dreamt that his body was in a vortex. He wasn't sure whether it was comprised of air or water, but something was definitely dragging him toward an abyss. He had to will himself to wake up because if he didn't, he sensed he would have never regained consciousness.

Frank felt someone tugging on his arm. He screamed and bolted upright.

"It's okay, Frank. It's okay," Max said. "It's only me."

"What are you doing here?" Frank asked.

"I've been calling you for hours. I thought something must have happened to you so I had the concierge let me in. He's waiting by the door."

"Tell him to go away." Frank tried to clear his head. "What time is it, anyway?"

"It's five in the afternoon."

"Jesus. I've slept for over twelve hours! I've got to get going. I have a show to do."

"Will you relax?" Max said. "Today is Monday."

Frank headed for the bathroom. He splashed some water on his face and took a look in the mirror. His face lacked color and he was a little drawn, but other than that, he seemed to be okay.

"Did you hear what I said?" Max repeated. "Today is Monday."

When Frank reentered the bedroom, Max was standing by the door. "I heard you, Max," Frank said. "You don't have to shout."

"But I'm not shouting."

"It must be my head. It hurts like hell."

"Do you want me to leave?"

"No, no. I want you to stay."

"You hypnotized yourself, didn't you?" It was more of a statement than a question.

"Yeah. I guess."

"What's it like?"

Frank sat on the edge of the bed. "I can't even begin to tell you. It was as if some power energized me. I remember thinking clearer. It was as if the mysteries of the universe had suddenly been revealed."

A look of concern crossed Max's face. "Mysteries of the universe? My God, Frank, don't you see what has happened?"

"Don't go there, Max. I don't want you to expound upon your philosophical thoughts, particularly about those damned akashic records."

Max gave Frank a look of concern. "Maybe you shouldn't read from that book."

Frank placed a hand on the grimoire. "I'll use it, but whenever I do, I'd like you to be around. Promise me you will never leave me alone when I am in a . . ."

"Trance?" Max volunteered.

"Yah, I guess that's what it was."

"I promise."

"I was so tired. So very, very tired, but now I'm afraid if I go to sleep, I might not wake up." Frank grabbed Max's arm. "You must promise me you won't let me sleep too long. And whatever happens, you won't leave me alone."

"I won't leave you alone. Go back to sleep."

Like a rush of wind, the tenseness left Frank. He lay back down on the bed and relaxed. When he woke up an hour later, Max was still there. "I don't know what I'd do without you," Frank said. "You truly are a good friend."

Max started to respond, but then stopped. What was there to say? For all these years he had depended on others, mainly Dottie. For the first time in his life, someone needed him. It was a great feeling, a feeling he wouldn't exchange for all the money in the world.

CHAPTER 26

It took Max only a few days to realize that Frank was undergoing some drastic changes, changes he was certain were being caused by the grimoire. Many were physical, but he had also noted some psychological differences in his personality. There was no doubt Frank was aging. The veins in his arms and legs were now varicosed and there were liver spots on his hands, the spots that suddenly appear on people in their late sixties. His hair, which was a lot greyer, had lost some of its luster. And then there were all those wrinkles. It made Frank's face look like it had been sculpted by a special-effects wizard. He had also started to walk with a slight stoop.

It seemed the more time Frank spent with the book, the frailer he became. But unlike his body, which was rapidly deteriorating, his mind was as sharp as ever. He had also become paranoid. Frank was convinced everyone from the bellhop to the parking lot attendant was conspiring against him. Max also noticed that Frank was avoiding Dottie. He knew his sister well. She had certainly had enough practice at worming her way into a man's heart. In the past, she would use her femininity to get what she wanted. All she would have to do is nibble on Frank's ear or stroke his cheek, and he would turn to gel. But even before he had moved out of the house, that kind of foreplay no longer worked.

Frank stopped seeing Dottie altogether when he moved into the Boulevardier. At first he would return her calls, but as of late, he never bothered to pick up the phone. Upon Dottie's insistence, Max had asked Frank why he had cut her out of his life.

"Look at me," Frank said. I'm forty-eight years old, and I look thirty years older. Dottie is twenty-eight. Do you think for a minute she would want to be with a man who looks old enough to be her grandfather?"

"What should I tell her?" Max had asked. "She has to be told something."

"Tell her I have some problems I need to resolve. Tell her I don't love her anymore. But, whatever you do, I don't want you to tell her the real reason. I know Dottie. She'd want to stick by me, and believe me, a week or two from now, I'll look even worse. You've got to remember I was forty-seven and she was twenty-seven when we got married. She's going to find me repulsive, if not now, then later. I don't think I'd be able to bear that."

Max felt sorry for his sister, but his allegiance was to Frank. His brother-in-law needed him. He had said so himself. Besides, Dottie was a survivor. One way or another, she would make it. Max recalled that by the time she had finished high school, she had become an accomplished dancer. She might have started at that strip joint his fellow high school students had called the "tittie bar," but she had somehow managed to rise above all that. It wasn't easy to land a job in a chorus line for a casino, particularly one on the Strip. Then, when Frank married her, she quit. Max didn't respect his sister for having used Frank. He told Frank as much, but Frank just shrugged. "Everybody uses everybody, Max," he had said, and then changed the subject.

Max stopped dwelling on the past and started thinking about the present. He had promised Frank he would take care of him, and he had meant every word. What worried him was Frank had become so preoccupied with the grimoire that between the book and his show, they seldom had a chance to talk. Frank would no longer set foot in his house. If he needed or wanted something, he'd ask Max to get it for him. Max didn't mind sleeping on the floor next to Frank's bed, but Frank had insisted on renting a two-bedroom suite. He seldom left his bedroom and only did so when he had to put on a show or when Max would force him to take a walk to get some fresh air.

Yesterday, Dottie had given Max a note and asked him to deliver it to Frank. He had to give his sister some credit. She refused to believe that Frank no longer loved her, and she was determined to see him. Although Max had told her the note wouldn't change Frank's mind, he had promised her he would deliver it.

In the newer Vegas hotels anyone wanting to go to their room had to pass through the casino. The Boulevardier was no exception. Max was walking toward the bank of elevators when he noticed a large crowd had formed at one of the crap tables nearby. Curious, he approached the table for a better look. He was surprised to see Frank rolling the dice. Actually, controlling the dice would be a more accurate description. Every time he'd throw the cubes, there would be a roar.

Max edged his way closer to the table so he could observe the action. He had to admit that Frank had not only mastered the technique of manipulating the dice, but he was also doing a pretty good job of acting as well. Frank purposely placed large bets when he wanted to win and small ones when he wanted to lose. He hardly showed any emotion when he won, but he would moan and groan whenever the croupier would sweep Frank's chips to his side of the felt-lined table.

The way Max figured, Frank was just getting even. He had been losing money for years at the Boulevardier, and now it was his turn to win. He walked up and handed him Dottie's note.

Frank crumpled it up and placed it in his pocket.

"Aren't you even going to read it?" Max whispered.

"Maybe later."

When the two of them were in the elevator, Max had asked him the same question.

"Read what?"

"Dottie's note."

"You are a persistent cuss."

"Come on, Frank. She is your wife, you know."

"No."

"What shall I tell her?"

"Tell her the truth. Tell her I threw it away."

"But that's mean-spirited, Frank."

"Maybe so, but it beats the alternative." They were in the hall walking toward their suite when Frank changed the subject. "Are you feeling lucky?"

"You know I don't gamble."

Frank laughed. "I don't either." When Frank said that, Max started to laugh, too.

Frank opened the door to his room. "Right now I need to get some rest. That was hard work what I was doing down there."

Max laughed. When he walked into his bedroom, he phoned Dottie.

"What do you mean he didn't read my note?" she asked.

"At first he said he would. I think he just forgot."

She started to cry. "It's that damned book, isn't it?"

"He hasn't been himself. There is a lot on his plate at the moment. Stover has been breathing down his neck. He's afraid his contract might not be renewed. I'd give him some space. Maybe once he figures out what kind of a show he's going to put on, he'll come around." Max wasn't sure if he was saying those things for his sister's benefit or for his own.

CHAPTER 27

Although Giuseppe couldn't find a record of Archbishop Dominique's execution, he did find the next best thing. It was a terse statement from the Vatican that had been included in a one-page release that the Roman Curia routinely made available to the citizens of Rome. Even after Giuseppe had read the short paragraph, he still had difficulty believing that the Vatican High Court had made good on its promise. Written in Latin and signed by some bureaucrat from the judiciary branch, it simply stated that the sentence of death by hanging imposed by the Vatican High Court on Archbishop Alberto Dominique for killing Father Simon Anglacio had been carried out on the morning of January 14, 1638, in front of three witnesses.

Two things immediately popped into Giuseppe's head. Where did this alleged execution take place and who were the witnesses? Since Giuseppe knew no one had ever been put to death within the Vatican's walls, much less a priest, he figured the event must have occurred elsewhere. The most logical place would be somewhere in Rome, but where? Then he realized if Archbishop Dominique had actually been hanged, there had to be a record of the execution. The clerk at the courthouse where such records were kept was only too anxious to help a cardinal, particularly one who was in charge of the Secret Archives.

Since the alleged execution had taken place centuries ago, Giuseppe was led to a storeroom where he spent several hours searching through index cards of those who had suffered the supreme penalty. But Dominique's name was not among those who had been put to death at the hands of an executioner. He even cross-checked the files by date of entry and discovered that no one was executed in Rome on the day of January 16, 1638, much less an archbishop.

As much as he wanted to pursue this further, there were other pressing matters to attend to. Carlotta had called to tell him that Antonio had received his email regarding the Punta Dora investment. She said Antonio wanted to talk to him personally, and hoped he could come for dinner. She suggested he dress casually as there would be just the three of them. Giuseppe had tried to come up with an excuse so he wouldn't have to go. He was sure Antonio would ask him to reconsider loaning him the money. Giuseppe wanted to avoid an altercation as he wasn't about to change his mind.

In retrospect, Giuseppe should have never encouraged his sister to marry Antonio. In the beginning, he had thought Antonio was a good provider. It was only after they were married that he discovered Antonio had cashed in his father's stock and invested the money in several hotels. Because he had paid cash for the hotels, his investments were making money, but Antonio began to expand. He mortgaged the hotels so he could enlarge his real estate holdings. Against his advice, he had continued to buy properties without giving any thought to cash reserves. When the economy soured, he was forced to borrow from the banks as he didn't have the cash to weather the storm. Even Giuseppe had loaned him some money. Antonio paid it back, but his real estate investment in Punta Dora made Giuseppe realize that Antonio hadn't learned from his mistakes.

But he had to admit that although Antonio might not have been an astute businessman, he had taken it upon himself to do everything he could to make him the next pope. For that reason, Giuseppe felt he owed him the courtesy of a meeting so in the end, he accepted the dinner invitation. After all, Carlotta was his sister, and as her older brother, he felt a familial obligation to be there at this difficult time.

The dinner began on a cordial note. The grappa was excellent as usual and Giuseppe laughed at Antonio's stories, even though they weren't funny. After they had dessert, Antonio led Giuseppe to the den where Giuseppe had begged off on a glass of cognac because of an early meeting with the pope.

"I received your email about the Punta Dora project," Antonio said. "I didn't particularly like your insinuations about my good friend Justin Saunders."

The last thing Giuseppe wanted was a scene. "As you know, Carlotta is powerless to lend you money from her share of the trust. I am the only one who can make such a decision."

"But you don't really know all of the ramifications of this deal," Antonio countered.

"I know what I emailed you was a lot more than insinuations. I also know if you put more money into that project, you are a bigger fool than I thought. Didn't you read what I sent you? The man is playing you. He wants you to lose the money you've already put in. Then all he has to do is step in and take over the entire project."

"Justin Saunders is a friend!" Antonio said in a raised voice. "He wouldn't do that to me."

"I think I had better go. As I said, I have an early meeting with the pope."

Suddenly, Antonio did an about-face. "You have to help me, Giuseppe." He was pleading now. Actually, it was more like groveling. "I didn't tell Carlotta this, but I ended up mortgaging the villa. If I get squeezed out of the Punta Dora project, I'll lose everything!"

Giuseppe couldn't believe what he was hearing. "Carlotta told me about the hotels. You also mortgaged the villa? This villa?"

"Please, don't tell Carlotta!" Antonio pleaded. "Unless I can come up with a payment in thirty days, the banks will foreclose."

"How could you do this to her?" Giuseppe asked in disgust. "It was hers. You gave it to her. You had no right!"

The look on Antonio's face convinced Giuseppe that this was a desperate man. "I don't know what came over me. Things got out of hand."

"How much is the mortgage on the house?" Giuseppe asked.

"A million euros."

Giuseppe didn't swear, but he was tempted to rattle off a few choice words. Instead, he walked toward the door. "I am sorry, Antonio. I cannot help you this time. Say good night for me to Carlotta, will you?"

Giuseppe knew he would never allow the bank to take the villa. He would pay off the loan himself and take title to the property in the name of the trust. But he wasn't about to tell Antonio that. Antonio had to be taught a lesson. And if it meant he would end up going bankrupt, then so be it. Maybe he would become a better person for it.

CHAPTER 28

A week after Frank had moved the two of them into the suite at the Boulevardier, Max had asked what it cost.

"What do you care?" was Frank's retort.

"I'm just curious, that's all."

"Fifteen hundred a night if you must know." Frank had said as if it were mere chump change.

Max had been flabbergasted. "Fifteen hundred a night. That's over ten thousand dollars a week, a ridiculous amount of money. I know I'm your caregiver as well as a friend, but you certainly don't need to spend that kind of money on my account."

"If you want to know the truth, I'm not paying for it; the Boulevardier is."

"I know when you put your mind to it, you can win as much money as you want or need, but fifteen hundred a night?"

"You worry too much," Frank had said and then changed the subject.

But Max had been right. Whenever he needed to make money, he'd go to one of the casinos and come back with a pile of cash. By gambling for an hour or so a day, he had managed to pay off all the money he owed to the casinos, every last cent. Now that he wasn't starved for cash, he gambled a lot less. In the beginning, before he had learned how to use the grimoire, he gambled because it had been exciting. Now that he could win anytime he wanted to, it was no longer any fun.

Frank was at the suite trying to rest up before the evening's performance when Max opened his bedroom door. "Sorry to disturb you, but Richard Stover is on the line. I told him to call back later, but he is very insistent. He says it's important."

"All right," Frank grunted. "Thanks, Max. I'll take the call."

Stover's voice grated in his ear. "I am getting tired of you giving me the runaround. You are supposed to meet with the hotel brass in two days. I've called you repeatedly, but you haven't bothered to return any of my calls. What is it with you? Do you have a death wish or something? Either you have a new show or you don't. Now which is it, for Christ's sake?"

Richard Stover no longer intimidated Frank. "I'll put on a show when I'm good and ready," he said.

There was some sputtering on the other end of the line. Then Stover said, "You can forget about having your contract renewed. I'm going to recommend to the principals of the Boulevardier that we hire a new headliner. I'll see to it you never get another job. At least not in Vegas."

"Threaten me for all I care. I know your kind. You are acting like a bulldozer gone berserk. Always pushing, always intimidating. Chill out, why don't you?"

Stover's harsh voice could have cut through lead. "What did you just say?"

"You heard me. Chill out! All you are and all you will ever be is a little man with a big ego. A month from now, when my new show is ready, I'll invite everybody who is a somebody in this town to a very special performance. I'll extend an invitation to all of those mucky mucks from the Boulevardier. And, if you're lucky, I might even invite you. Once the movers and shakers see my show, I'll be able to write my own ticket . . . and you'll get the sack for not having had the foresight to renew my contract."

Frank disconnected before Stover had a chance to respond. He was confident that within a short period of time, he would be able to lift himself three or four feet off the ground. But in addition to a levitation act, he was in the process of formulating something very special. And, if he could pull it off, every entertainment director in Las Vegas would be after him. Money no longer motivated him. Hell, he could get as much cash as he needed or wanted in other ways.

Frank knew he would always have the upper hand . . . as long as he had the grimoire.

CHAPTER 29

Giuseppe was in his office when one of the priests assigned to the Secret Archives knocked on the door. "I hate to disturb you, Your Eminence, but I came across some files that deal with 'actions' for which indulgences have been granted. I thought I would bring them to your attention as I didn't know how you would want to handle them."

Giuseppe took his eyes off the manuscript he had been scrutinizing. He was well aware that in the past, much like gelato vendors, the Catholic Church would sell indulgences. If a person had enough money, lenience for one's spirit could be bought regardless of the severity of the crime. It was much like purchasing an insurance policy. Although the Church had no power or authority to pardon a criminal act, an indulgence could save a person's soul from going to hell.

Giuseppe turned toward the priest. "I'm not interested in personally reviewing every indulgence the Vatican has arranged. Thousands must have been sold to raise money to build the Basilica."

"I am sorry, Your Eminence, I wasn't talking about those kinds of indulgences. I was referring to permanent absolutions that had been granted to members of the clergy either by the apostolic penitentiary or by a supreme tribunal."

Giuseppe didn't fault the priest because he knew the Church would often use words such as "actions" because they sounded less offensive than a "sin" or a "crime." Giuseppe also knew that although the apostolic penitentiary the priest had referred to had been replaced in modern times by what was now called the ecumenical penitentiary, the function of the penitentiaries was exactly the same. "So what you are saying is the absolution for these indulgences are at least two hundred years old?"

"Yes, Your Eminence. That's another reason I wanted to bring the matter to your attention. Most penitents sought forgiveness for minor offenses. You would most likely agree that files of this nature should remain here, in the Secret Archives. But what about serious infractions committed by members of the clergy? Offenses such as defiling the Eucharist. Canonical offenses that unless absolution was granted, would most likely bring about excommunication from the Church."

Giuseppe hated long-winded conversations. "So what's your point?"

"I thought Your Eminence would want to review those files personally. Some are . . . rather delicate if I may use such a word. I thought much of this material might be more appropriately placed in the Room of Dark Secrets."

Giuseppe smiled. Here was a young priest who had somehow managed to find out that such a room existed. He reminded Giuseppe of himself twenty years ago. The priest would most likely be a bishop one day, maybe even a cardinal. "How many absolutions are we talking about?"

"Oh, not that many. I would venture to say a couple of hundred, maybe less. If you like, I could . . ."

"No. You did the right thing by bringing these files to my attention. Would it be possible for you to have them brought here, to my office?

"Most certainly. They'll be here by tomorrow morning."

By the time Giuseppe arrived in his office, after morning Mass, the files had been neatly stacked on the floor beside his desk. He picked up the first one. Unfortunately, priests had just as many faults as the parishioners who brought their confessions to them. One penitent asked for forgiveness after he had performed an abortion. Another had sex with a woman and then offered her forgiveness for the act. Then there was the priest who had broken the confidence of the confessional, which Giuseppe thought was the most despicable thing a man of the cloth could do.

The list went on and on. After a couple of hours of tedious work sorting through priests' misdeeds, he began to tire of it all. Most of the offenses took place two to four hundred years ago, and some were a lot older than that. He was about to ask one of his assistants to sort through them when he ran across a file different from the others. It's not often a man of the Church asks for absolution after committing murder.

Providence certainly worked in strange ways. What he had in front of him was a request for mercy from one Archbishop Alberto Dominique, the very same man who had been tried, convicted and sentenced to die at the gallows . . . and supposedly had been executed.

It didn't make sense. The trial and ultimately the verdict of Archbishop Dominique had been made public. Based on canonical law, the Prefect of the Apostolic Penitentiary did not have the authority to grant absolution in cases when the public had been made aware of the offense. Yet, the decision of the tribunal was quite clear. Archbishop Dominique had been granted mercy, but what had made it even worse was the cardinal who had arranged the absolution for Dominique had done so at a time of *sede vacante*.

The bile from Giuseppe's stomach rose to his throat. "This cannot be!" He had uttered the words so loud that one of the priests came in to make sure he was all right. Giuseppe waved him off. Not many people outside the Catholic Church even knew what the words *sede vacante* meant. A Prefect of the Apostolic Penitentiary had the authority to grant clemency, even in the interim between a time when the old pope had died and a new one had not yet been chosen. But in the course of history, no member of the clergy ever received complete absolution for murder as no pope would have dared to grant one. Normally, when a priest was found guilty of committing a heinous crime such as murder, he would be excommunicated from the Church. But not Archbishop Dominique. He was demoted to a priest and sent to a small parish on the outskirts of Marseilles, France.

Giuseppe now knew why the grimoire's documents had been shrouded in such secrecy. His mind was in a tailspin. "The audacity of those people," he blurted. "No wonder so many think our Church is corrupt." Just then a horrid thought entered his mind. What if someone were to divulge all of this information to the public? He could read the headlines now:

PRIEST'S EXECUTION SECRETLY STAYED

CHURCH GRANTS MERCY TO MURDEROUS
ARCHBISHOP

PEOPLE OF ROME DECEIVED!

Even though the blasphemous act had occurred centuries ago, Giuseppe felt that if such a scandal ever became known to the public, it would undermine the credibility of the Roman Catholic Church, a trustworthiness that had already been tested as of late by some rather scandalous cover-ups of unscrupulous activities performed by priests. To put it in simple terms, the Church had already received one black eye. It certainly did not need another.

To say that Giuseppe was shocked would have been an understatement. He was disgusted. In Giuseppe's eyes, a precedent had been set. If it ever became public knowledge within the Vatican that a member of the clergy was given absolution for murder by someone other than the pope himself, what was to prevent other prefects from granting similar requests?

What a mess! Fortunately this had all happened inside the Vatican, and even if the files were locked in the impenetrable Room of Dark Secrets, there was always the possibility of a leak.

Giuseppe felt there was only one thing to do. Those files had to destroyed, every last one of them.

CHAPTER 30

In the beginning, Frank would quit reading from the grimoire as soon as he felt the power's presence. But as time went on, he discovered that the longer he continued with the incantations, the more potent the force within him became.

Within a relatively short period of time, he learned how to use the energy of his mind to stop a roulette wheel on a predetermined number. He also figured out how to control the disks that spun inside slot machines.

Nothing gave him greater satisfaction than to walk through a casino and manipulate a series of slots so they would award their players with the ultimate prize, the granddaddy of all jackpots! The shrill sound a slot machine made when a player hit the jackpot would attract quite a bit of attention. It told others that perhaps, if they played long enough, that they, too, could walk away with more money than what they had started with. When ten or fifteen machines hit simultaneous jackpots, the sound was ear-bending. Frank enjoyed watching casino employees scatter in different directions in their attempt to pay off the winners.

Frank's mind still wasn't ready to tackle the movement of large objects from one place to another, but he knew if he kept at it that eventually he would reach his goal.

The headaches in between trances were not only becoming less frequent, but they were also less excruciating. The previous owner of the grimoir had committed a fatal mistake, a mistake he certainly did not wish to repeat. Jonathan Hollingsworth had pushed himself too hard, too fast. He had tried to accomplish more than what his mind was capable of enduring.

Frank hoped he would never have to cross the threshold of rational thought into an asylum of insanity. He wondered how the glory of one thing could so quickly become the horror of another.

* * *

Max Hunter should have been jubilant. As Frank's shadow, he was earning more money than he had ever imagined, but he was genuinely concerned for his brother-in-law. It wasn't just that Frank was becoming more paranoid. His body was continuing to age, and in a dramatical way. Only a week before, Max caught him dyeing the grey from his hair. Now he had hardly any hair at all. Frank's arms, which had once been muscular, were so thin Max thought his skin was resting on nothing but bone. There was a washed-out look about him, an unhealthy sallowness only very old people had.

Max was certain the force, which was now within Frank, was not only sapping his strength, but was extracting from him the very juices of life. Even if Max could somehow take the grimoire away from Frank, he knew his brother-in-law could never return to the way he had been before the book entered into his life. The damage was irreversible and Max felt totally powerless.

It was as if Frank had boarded a runaway train that sooner or later would collide with another one going in the opposite direction.

He wondered where Frank would be once the two trains met.

* * *

It was a Monday night, the only night Frank wasn't performing. The two were in the suite's spacious living room watching television when there was a persistent knock on the door.

"See who it is, will you, Max?" Frank said.

Max was afraid it might be Dottie. The last thing he wanted was for her to create a scene. He opened the door, but no Dottie. Instead, a man in a messenger's uniform was at the door. "Are you Frank Santino?" the man asked.

"No. I'm his brother-in-law."

"Is Mister Santino staying here?"

"Yes," Frank said. "What's this about?"

"Hey, I'm just a messenger." After handing Max an envelope, the man gave him something to sign.

Max took a step back.

"It's not a bomb," the messenger said. "I just need your signature. It means I delivered it."

After he signed and the messenger left, Max took a look at the envelope. The only thing on it was Frank's name. He walked over to Frank and handed it to him. "This is for you."

"It's probably some ultimatum from that S.O.B. Stover." He tore the envelope open and glanced at the note. Then he crumpled it and threw it in the trash.

"Was it from Stover?" Max asked.

"No. It was from Dottie. I swear that woman won't give up."

"Maybe you should see her," Max suggested.

Frank couldn't help but laugh. "Look at me. If she saw the way I look, it would freak her out. No. The best thing for me to do is to just ignore her. Sooner or later she'll get tired of being rejected. When that happens, she'll divorce me."

"Come on, Frank. At least write to her or call her."

Frank didn't answer Max for quite some time. Finally, he said, "Why prolong the inevitable?" Then he quickly changed the subject. "Come one, let's finish watching the game. Once it's over, I'm going to bed. I know it's early, but I'm beat. Tomorrow will be a long day."

"What's happening tomorrow?" Max asked.

"Tomorrow is the first day of my rebirth."

"And what's that supposed to mean?"

"I am going to lift myself off the ground."

CHAPTER 31

Since his altercation with Antonio, Giuseppe had received yet another dinner party invitation from Carlotta, the second in a week. He knew he could no longer beg off with the excuse he had too much work to do. He accepted this one with the caveat that it would have to be an early evening.

Because the pope was much too ill to discuss matters pertaining to the Church, Giuseppe had requested to see Cardinal Callistus who was the Prefect of the Ecumenical Penitentiary. Because of the pope's incapacitation, Callistus was not only the third-highest ranking member of the Catholic Church, but he was one of Giuseppe's mentors and had often offered words of encouragement to him when he was an archbishop. Giuseppe was granted an audience with the cardinal and was reviewing the notes he had taken about the cover-up in preparation for the meeting. He had taken great pains to summarize the entire chain of events leading to the conspiracy. He chose to do this because he was forbidden to remove any original files from either the Secret Archives or from the Room of Dark Secrets, unless, of course, he had the pope's permission.

Because Cardinal Callistus was authorized to act in a pope's absence, Giuseppe was going to recommend to him that all records in reference to Archbishop Dominique be destroyed. After all, the principals in the scheme had been dead for quite some time so why keep files that could come back to haunt the Church?

He took another quick look, and then placed the information he had written inside his briefcase. Once that was accomplished, he rushed off to meet with the cardinal. When he arrived at the office of the ecumenical penitentiary, he was informed by the cardinal's secretary that Cardinal Callistus was detained on a matter of extreme urgency and that he would return to meet with him as soon as possible.

Giuseppe was on his third magazine when the cardinal's secretary approached him. "I am very sorry, Cardinal Mercati, but

Cardinal Callistus won't be able to see you till tomorrow. Would you mind meeting with him over breakfast?"

Giuseppe tried not to show his anger. He had wanted to shower and change clothes, and now there wasn't enough time. It was already five thirty, and he had promised Carlotta he would be at the villa by six. He would be late, but then he never arrived at a party or dinner engagement on time. He summoned his driver and told him to drive to the villa.

A servant opened the front door, and moments later Carlotta arrived. She looked as beautiful as ever. "I am so glad you could come, Giuseppe. It looks like the two of us will be dining alone. Antonio is not feeling well. It's probably a touch of the flu. He told me tonight would be one of the few nights you wouldn't have to put up with his jokes."

Giuseppe was relieved. He probably figured Antonio wanted some time to pass before the two saw one another and that was just fine with him. At least he wouldn't have to listen to his money problems.

He handed his sister the briefcase. "I have some important papers here. Would you mind putting my case in your safe?"

"Not at all. Make yourself at home. Why don't we have our drinks in the family room?"

Carlotta did most of the talking, but Giuseppe didn't mind for he was a good listener. He waited for Carlotta to mention the difficulties Antonio was having with the Punta Dora project, but his sister had skirted away from talking about Antonio altogether. She brought Giuseppe up to date on the many charitable events she was sponsoring and also mentioned she planned to travel with Antonio to the United States to check on some potential land he was thinking of purchasing for a new hotel in California. Giuseppe assumed Antonio's setback had just been temporary and that he had managed to place his financial house in order.

After drinking more grappa than he had intended, he asked Carlotta to fetch his briefcase and had his driver take him back to his apartment at the Vatican.

While in the car, Giuseppe opened the briefcase and once more reviewed the material he would be discussing with Cardinal Callistus over breakfast the next morning.

* * *

Giussepe was on time for his breakfast meeting with Callistus, in fact, he was a few minutes early. He was pleased he only had to refer to his notes a couple of times while talking to the cardinal. Once Giuseppe had finished, he reiterated the reason he was recommending that all paperwork that dealt with the conspiracy be destroyed.

"It is a different world we are living in now, Cardinal," he told Callistus. "If any of this information were to leak out, it could cause a global-wide scandal, a scandal our Church doesn't need." Then he added, "Particularly when we are undergoing such difficult times." Guiseppe thought the statement was general enough and could be interpreted in many different ways, which had been his intent.

Cardinal Callistus appeared to give some thought to what Giuseppe had just told him. "To my knowledge no Cardinal Elector in the history of the Church has given a murderer absolution without first consulting with a pope. What I am referring to is absolution of the soul. But in this case, Archbishop Dominique had been given an unequivocal pardon, a pardon that the Church was not authorized to give. You say you actually saw a letter of absolution signed by the Prefect of the Ecumenical Penitentiary? And the letter pardoned this archbishop before a new pope had been elected even though the population of Rome had heard about the incident?"

"That is correct. Not only did the cardinal pardon Archbishop Dominique, but he took it upon himself to demote him and had him transferred to a parish outside of Marseilles, France. Just so you know, he had taken this drastic course of action right after the pope had died."

"Holy Mother of God, the man must have been mad! This cardinal violated the very principles the apostolic penitentiary has been founded on. We operate in secrecy; I am certain you know that. To pardon a cleric who had committed such a horrific crime goes against all principles of canonic law. And to do so without giving a pope the final say in the matter is simply disgusting."

"That's what I thought you would say. As you know, our pope is gravely ill. That's why I wanted you to know what I had uncovered. I thought you might want to have the material destroyed."

Cardinal Callistus was so taken aback that he slammed the back of his head into the headrest of his chair. "Do you realize what you are saying, Giuseppe? You are asking me to do the same thing the Prefect of the Apostolic Penitentiary did in the seventeenth century, and that is to usurp a pope's authority! I am surprised you would even suggest such a thing." Callistus stood. As there was no one else in the dining room, he began to pace. "I cannot in all good conscience do that."

"But as you know, the pope is on his deathbed," Giuseppe said. "Besides, it's not quite the same thing. All I am asking you to do is give me permission to destroy several files. You must remember the files I just spoke about are four hundred and fifty years old."

Callistus sat back down. "You still don't get it, do you? These secrets belong to the Church, and in a way to all the popes who had harbored them throughout the centuries. Only a pope can authorize their destruction."

Cardinal Callistus moved his breakfast dishes aside, a sure sign he wanted to conclude the meeting. "It's true. I do have the authority to act for the pope, either a dead one or one who is dying. And I would do so, but only in a case of extreme necessity. I see no urgency here. Those records have been in the Room of Dark Secrets for four hundred fifty years; certainly another month, even two, won't make any difference. Mind you, I am not minimizing the despicable deeds a number of high-ranking members of our Church had performed. But let us not forget that all of this took place a long, long time ago. I suggest you bring this matter up with the pope if and when he gets well. And if our Holy Father dies, then bring the matter to the new pope's attention, once one is elected."

Needless to say, Giuseppe was disappointed with Callistus's decision, but there was nothing he could do. He decided to have all the files as well as the notes he had taken transferred to the Room of Dark Secrets. He locked the door and vowed not to reenter until a new pope made a decision as to what should be done with the material that most certainly would cause an international scandal if the cover-up ever got into the hands of some unscrupulous person.

Giuseppe vowed if he were to be elected pope, the first thing he would do is have the files destroyed.

What he still hoped to find was the location of the grimoire. He had so much wanted to have a look at a book that had caused one member of the clergy to kill another.

CHAPTER 32

Frank Santino could now enter a possessory trance within a few minutes. He still suffered headaches afterwards, but they only lasted for a short period of time. He learned how to vacate his mind of all superfluous thoughts, which enabled him to channel all of his energy toward one aim. The power was there; what he needed to do was learn how to use it more effectively. So he practiced.

He established a daily routine and asked Max to help him make sure he stuck to it. The first thing he would do was his yoga exercises. Then, he'd focus on a stack of books and one by one move them from one location of the room to another. He became so adept at it that he could move as many as a couple dozen at one time.

Once he finished the exercises, Max would bring him some breakfast, a meal he would have to force himself to eat. Although he knew most of the phrases by heart, he would spend some time reading passages from the grimoire. Frank found that the book gave him the confidence to push himself deeper and deeper into a trance-like meditative state, a state he was sure was an extension of his soul.

A week ago, he had asked Max to buy him a three-foot garden statue made of pressed concrete. He would spend twenty minutes a day, no more and no less, focusing his mind on the statue. He'd envision the figurine lifting from the floor and floating on a cloud of air. At first, he could only move the heavy object a few inches off the ground. But he kept at it until he could lift it four feet off the floor.

A month had passed before Frank felt he was ready for a more difficult challenge. He had a special metal cage built to his exact requirements. The enclosure was large enough to house a couple of large dogs. The cage, which consisted of a top, a floor, and four sides, could be separated by the removal of several steel rods. When it was intact, it was a prison that no animal could escape from. But when he willed it to separate, all the pieces would come crashing to the floor.

After working with an empty cage for over a week, Frank was ready to tackle the next and most difficult part of the exercise. It was one thing to move a stationary object around a room using the power of one's mind and quite another to hold a living, breathing animal in place in midair.

He rented a small, empty warehouse where he could practice his routines. He started with a rabbit. Although he taught himself how to dismantle the cage with his mind, he couldn't get the knack of "freezing" the animal in midair. The minute the cage would fall apart, the startled rabbit would end up on the ground.

Max tried to dissuade Frank. "You have already learned how to move objects around a room. Not only that, but you have also mastered the art of levitation. My God, Frank, you can now lift yourself off the ground. What more do you want?"

"It's not enough," Frank said. "I can do this, Max. I know I can." What Frank needed was patience. It had been on the tip of his tongue to ask Max how he had acquired the tolerance to stay immobile for long periods of time when he had been a sniper, but then thought better of it. There was no sense in dredging up Max's past, at least not right now.

Frank decided he was probably rushing things a bit, so he bought some mice. He'd toss them in the air one at a time over a mattress and would try to freeze them in space. When that didn't work, he had Max attach a string to their tails. At a prearranged signal, Frank would have Max let go of the string. That also didn't work.

He was about to give up, when he thought of another idea. He recalled the day he had first entered into a possessory trance. The lights had gone out. He had been forced to recite from the grimoire using the light from the Zippo. Frank had Max cover the warehouse windows with black butcher paper. He then had him light four candles and place one in each corner of the room. The candles generated just barely enough light for Frank to focus on a mouse. He formed a mental picture of the creature hovering in space. The instant Max let go of the string, much to Frank's amazement and

Max's surprise, the mouse dangled in midair right in front of them. It could twitch its nose and move its paws, but other than that, it was immobile.

That was a major breakthrough. From that point on, it didn't take Frank long to perform the same feat with a rabbit. From a rabbit, Frank went to a cat, and then to a mid-sized dog. He knew he was ready once he was able to freeze a one-hundred-eighty-pound Saint Bernard five feet off the ground for a four-minute stretch.

When Max saw the dog suspended in midair, he applauded. "I have to hand it to you, Frank. You did it!"

Frank smiled. "Call it the power of positive thinking." Having said those words, Frank collapsed. When he came to, Max helped him into the Ferrari. He drove around with the top down until Frank felt better.

"You shouldn't have tackled so much," Max had told him once they had returned to the suite. "I want you to take a couple of days off to rest. You are pushing yourself much too hard. Remember you always end up paying a price. You are going to have one hell of a headache when you wake up tomorrow."

Frank cringed. "I know, but I'd rather have one of my migraines than be a second-rate magician, which is what Stover thinks I am."

Max placed a damp cloth on Frank's forehead. "Regardless of what Stover thinks, you have never been a second-rate magician." Max pulled up a chair next to Frank. "Whether you think so or not, the illusions you perform are extraordinary, but what you can do now goes way beyond that." Max seemed to grope for the right words. "I've learned something from all of this."

"What's that?

"The mind is a remarkable thing. I firmly believe human beings are capable of accomplishing feats that are . . . I was going to say paranormal, but then I'm not sure what you do is even that. What I do know is you have raised the benchmark of what humans can accomplish."

Frank went to the safe where he kept the grimoire. He took out a document and handed it to Max. "I want you to keep this. It's a copy of my will. It stipulates that Dottie is to get the house and half of everything else I own. You are to get the other half . . . and the grimoire."

Max was so taken by Frank's generosity that he had to fight back tears. Once he composed himself, he said, "You will outlive me, you old fox. I know you will."

Max heard the sadness in Frank's voice. "Maybe I will, but in case I don't, at least I know you won't have any financial worries." Frank placed both of his hands on Max's shoulders. "I want you to know I could have never done this without you. You have become more to me than just a distant relative. Before I really got to know you, I thought of you simply as Dottie's younger brother. But not anymore." Tears welled up in Frank's eyes. "You are the best friend anyone could possibly have."

"If you could just try to back off a little, Frank. That would make me so happy."

Frank shook his head. "We wouldn't be here in this place right now if Columbus had listened to his crew. Whenever a man decides to sail in uncharted waters, there is always the danger he might not return. I, for one, am willing to face the risk."

The serious expression on Frank's face melted into a smile. "Look at it this way. If my time does come, at least I'll go out in style."

CHAPTER 33

Giuseppe was in his office when the call came. The dean of the Sacred College was on the line. "I have sad news. I've just been informed by the Prefect of the Pontifical Household that the Holy Father has passed away."

Giuseppe had known for quite some time that the pope's condition had been terminal; nonetheless, he was saddened by the news. There was much to be done. Giuseppe knew only too well that the minute the pope died, his ecclesiastical jurisdiction came to an end, and so did his job as Prefect of the Secret Archives. The only thing he could do now was make sure he followed the protocol set forth in the Apostolic Constitution.

He handed in his resignation as well as the key to the Room of Dark Secrets to the Carmerlengo who oversees all property belonging to the Holy See. Had he not been given the key to the Room of Dark Secrets, he could have handed in his written resignation to the Vicar, whose job is to act in the pope's behalf. However, under the circumstances, the proper thing to do was to give the key to the Carmerlengo. He was well aware that his resignation from the prestigious job as Prefect of the Secret Archives was merely a formality. The chances were the new pontiff, whoever that might be, would ask him to continue the job of making some order out of the chaos that existed in the place.

And then it dawned on him. What if he were to become pope? A rush of adrenalin coursed through him. Was that just a pipe dream or could that become a reality? Some fairly influential people seemed to think he had a chance. At fifty-five, many would say he was too young to assume such an awesome responsibility. That, he knew, was the old school of thought, for age did not make a person wise. All age did was increase the chances of senility.

He didn't dwell long on the matter as there was still so much to do. After informing all the priests who worked under his supervision of the pope's death, he was free to perform the most important job a cardinal had to do, and that was to participate in the election process of a new pope.

Giuseppe decided his odds of becoming a pope were rather slim. There would be many Cardinal Electors who would want to choose someone older, someone who would still want to cling to the age-old traditions of the Church. Giuseppe guessed some electors wouldn't consider him to be spiritual enough to become a pope. He felt this was because unlike a number of the older cardinals, he wouldn't be adverse to changing some of the traditions of the Church. Not that he would ever discuss this openly, but he always felt it was ridiculous that priests were not allowed to marry. His position was that if a parish priest could have a wife and children, he would be in a better position to understand some of the familial problems so many congregationalists faced.

It was well known throughout the Vatican that Giuseppe placed a high value on the administrative process. He equated a pope's position with that of a CEO. He often told Carlotta that in this modern age, diplomacy was just as important as spiritual leadership. A few called him an opportunist. In a way, they were right. Giuseppe believed in seizing the moment, but not for power and glory. Had he wanted those things, he would have remained in the private sector.

No, Giuseppe wanted to become a pope because he truly believed he could make a difference. To his way of thinking, millions of parishioners, good Catholics all, had strayed from the fold because there were too many priests who still gave fire and brimstone sermons from their pulpits. He felt the way to God's heart was through love, not fear.

He told himself now was not the time for philosophical conjecture. He gathered a few of his belongings and headed to the meeting where the Cardinal Electors would decide on funeral arrangements for the pontiff. From there, he would go to Saint Peter's Vatican Basilica with the other cardinals to celebrate the rites for the dead pontiff's soul.

* * *

Nine days later, when the rites had been carried out, Giuseppe entered the Sistine Chapel. He would remain there, sequestered with the other cardinals until a Supreme Pontiff had been chosen.

Upon entering the best-known chapel in the Apostolic Palace, Giuseppe couldn't help but admire the ceiling and walls, which had been frescoed by the greatest of the Renaissance artists including Michelangelo, Raphael, and Bermini. Although he had been in the chapel dozens of times, he was still in awe of its architecture. The pendentives, which permitted the placement of circular domes over the ceiling of the chapel, were evocative of Solomon's Temple as described in the Old Testament. This chapel, more than any other, has served as a place of religious activity for close to two thousand years.

Unlike some of the older cardinals, Giuseppe did not believe the next pope to be chosen would be due to heavenly intervention. To his way of thinking, God had too many other things to do than worry about who would become the next pope.

Being "locked in" the Sistine Chapel with the other Cardinal Electors gave him an opportunity to circulate among those cardinals he didn't know well. Not only did he make a point to greet them by name, but whenever possible, he would pay them a compliment. After all, wasn't this the best way to get votes?

CHAPTER 34

Cardinal Romanus was in the middle of having his lunch when he was told of the pontiff's death. Like Giuseppe, Romanus also resigned from his position as Prefect of the Vatican Library and after saying a prayer for the dead pontiff, he left to attend the procedural and ceremonial activities.

By the time he entered the Sistine Chapel, over half of the Cardinal Electors had already gathered. Once they were all present and accounted for, the Sacred Roman Rota, charged with the responsibility of keeping a watchful eye over everything that was brought to the conclave or taken from it, posted Papal Swiss Guards at all the entrances. At that point, the doors leading to the chapel were locked from the inside as well as the outside.

Having had the privilege of voting for a pope in the past, Romanus knew neither he nor the other cardinals would be allowed to speak to anyone from outside the conclave until a new pope was selected. Romanus watched the Master of Pontifical Ceremonies turn the congregation over to the Dean of the Sacred College of Cardinals who was to preside over the election.

A Mass followed. It was designed so each of the cardinals could pray for enlightenment from God as to whom among them would make the best pope.

The Dean walked up to the podium and addressed the conclave. "Let me remind you of the oath each and everyone of you took to preserve the secrecy of these proceedings. . . ."

As the Dean spoke, Romanus's eyes rested upon Cardinal Giuseppe Mercati. He knew that regardless of how the voting went he would never cast his vote for him. He crossed himself and asked God for forgiveness for Romanus knew that as a man of God, it was sinful to resent another human being, particularly a fellow cardinal. But Romanus could not help himself. He prayed to God that Mercati would not receive the two-thirds-plus-one majority vote required to become the leader of his beloved Church.

Romanus had his reasons. Giuseppe was everything Romanus was not. Unlike Giuseppe, Romanus had not come from an aristocratic family, nor did he attend prestigious schools as a youth. Compared to Mercati, Romanus led a simple life. He didn't hobnob with important people nor did he have an affinity for alcohol. Romanus had no living relatives and since he had become a cardinal, his entire life centered around prayer. Not only did he attend the obligatory Mass three times a day as did the other cardinals, but he also prayed privately to God for hours at a time, for he believed the Almighty was not only omniscient, but controlled every aspect of nature, human and otherwise.

Once a break in the proceedings was announced, Romanus's gaze focused on Mercati. What the cardinal was doing was distasteful. Mercati reminded him of a gadfly, running around glad-handing with the other cardinals.

Being that Romanus was not a politician, and not aspiring to be the next pope, he kept mostly to himself. Although he firmly believed that politics had no place in the Roman Catholic Church, he wasn't naïve enough to think that most cardinals who sought the job would refrain from networking. Although there were other cardinals besides Mercati who were trying to win votes, at least they were being subtle about it. Romanus felt their "politicking" would do them no good, as he happened to believe the Holy Spirit would guide them all toward the right decision, the most important decision.

CHAPTER 35

Frank Santino was backstage waiting to make his grand entrance. Normally, when he would greet an audience, they would show their appreciation with applause. But tonight was different. When he took off his hat and bowed, the gesture was met with silence. Because the spotlights were aimed right at him, he couldn't see the audience. Of course, that had its advantages as he didn't particularly want to see all those people watching his every move.

Frank shook off the cool reception and went right into his routine. Everything was going smoothly until one of the wires used to lift the top of the chest snapped. Embarrassingly, the lid to the chest swung lopsided in midair. Once the audience put two and two together the booing started. "Throw the bum out," he heard someone yell. "Get rid of the imposter," shouted another.

"Wait," Frank shouted back. "In a few weeks I'll have something new to show you. Something really different. Cut me some slack, will you?"

The stage manager ran out on the stage, grabbed Frank by the shoulders, and screamed loud enough for the audience to hear. "Stover told me to tell you that you are finished. Do you hear me? Finished!"

"Wake up, Frank, wake up." Frank opened his eyes to see Max standing over him. "Are you all right?" Max asked, his voice full of concern.

Frank sat up in bed, drenched in sweat. "Jesus, I must have been dreaming. What time is it?"

"It's three in the morning. Go back to sleep."

"No. I'll never be able to sleep. Go and get the grimoire, will you?"

"Frank, be reasonable. You need to rest. You haven't had a good night's sleep in over three weeks."

"Do as I ask. I want to be ready for my new show in a week, two at most.

"You already learned to levitate. Just the other day, you managed to lift yourself several feet off the ground."

"That's not high enough. I know I can do better."

"Why are you doing this? It's certainly not for the money. My God, Frank. You don't have to work another day in your life. All you have to do is walk into a casino and an hour later, you . . ."

Frank rested a hand on Max's shoulder. "It's not for the money."

"Then for what? Stover? You want to prove to him you can do what has never been done before? You're ten times the man he'll ever be."

"Yes, I want to show him and everyone else that I'm not a has-been, but mainly I am doing this for myself. Don't you see? I've drifted through life without accomplishing a damn thing. Hell, the show I do now isn't really mine. I just took over where another guy had left off. Sure, I made a few bucks, and for the most part, I've had a good time, but what I really want is to place a bookmark on a page somewhere in the annals of history. I want to be remembered for doing something that no one else has been able to do. That's what's really important to me. I've gone through life trying to please other people, my mother, my first wife, Dottie . . . and yes, even Richard Stover. I can't begin to describe the helplessness, the feeling of despair . . . of the thought of being a has-been."

"You have never been a has-been," Max said.

"Sometimes I think it would have been better if Stover would have never offered me a headliner's job. And because he had, I have to prove to myself that I have it in me to make this thing work. You don't know how many times I had envisioned myself working at some third-rate carney show, living out of a dilapidated trailer, drinking rotgut whisky, because that would be all I could afford."

Frank's frail body started to shake. "I'll be fifty soon. I couldn't have paid off my gambling debts had I not come across the grimoire. Can you imagine what would have happened to me if I would have lost my contract with the Boulevardier? It would have been a downhill slide all the way."

Frank wiped the perspiration off his forehead. "I hadn't told you this, but I passed a homeless person the other day. He was standing in front of a drugstore with an empty beer can with the top cut off in his hand, the poor, pathetic soul. He must have been seventy, maybe seventy-five."

Frank reached out towards Max. Anyone watching would have interpreted Frank's gesture as a cry for help. "The horror of it all was when I looked at that poor guy, sitting there all alone, it was as if I was looking at myself in the mirror ten, twenty years from now."

Max's eyes welled up with tears, his voice merely a whisper. "You are wrong about the part of being alone. You will never be alone. What scares me is that if you continue to push yourself like this, citing chants from that damned book, I'll be the one who will be alone."

Frank looked at Max as if he was seeing him for the first time. For this man, who at one point in time had snuffed out the lives of over seventy people, had more compassion, more empathy, more love, than anyone he had ever known. He closed his eyes. "I'm going to try and get some more sleep. You'll be around, won't you?

"I'll be around."

CHAPTER 36

Giuseppe took the triangular-shaped ballot he had been given and examined it. When he read the printed Latin words, a joy coursed through him that he would have been hard pressed to explain. For the words *"Eligo in Summum Pontificem"* was the start of a sentence which he was supposed to complete. "I choose as Supreme Pontiff . . ." He wrote down his name and prayed the other Cardinal Electors would do likewise.

When it was his turn, he folded the ballot in two and took it to the altar where the examiners were stationed. He knelt before the urn where he was supposed to place his vote and said a prayer, which was the custom. Then, in a loud voice so that all could hear, he recited the phrase he had been asked to memorize earlier:

"I call Christ the Lord, my judge, to witness that I am voting for the one whom, in the Lord, I think should be elected." He then placed the ballot on a plate. When an examiner was satisfied that only one ballot had been filled out, he was instructed to place it inside the urn. Giuseppe then bowed in front of the altar and returned to the place where he had been standing.

The entire voting process took hours to complete. Finally, when all of the ballots had been cast, Giuseppe stood transfixed and watched in anticipation as the examiners began their work. After the first and second examiner verified the accuracy of each ballot, a third examiner read each name in a clear, loud voice. Once the votes were tallied, using a needle, the third examiner threaded each of the ballots, knotted them in a bunch, and then placed them in an empty urn.

Giuseppe's heart raced with excitement every time the examiner read his name. Although he heard his name repeated on numerous occasions, it was much too premature for him to think he would be the one chosen. Other names besides his were also read. Although Giuseppe had lost track, he suspected he was one of a half dozen cardinals whose name had been mentioned more than a couple times. Although this was his first conclave, others told him that sometimes it took days, even weeks for a cardinal to receive two-thirds majority plus one additional vote.

Having been forewarned, it was no surprise when an examiner added a chemical compound to the first four strings of ballots and placed them in a stove and chimney that had been erected just for such a purpose. Although he couldn't see the smoke, he knew it was black, which told the thousands of people who had gathered in Saint Peter's square that a pope had not been chosen.

With each string of ballots burned, Giuseppe's name came up more and more frequently. It was as if providence had interceded in his behalf.

Would he reach the number of votes needed to win the election? He willed himself not to be overly optimistic, but it did appear he would be a strong contender.

* * *

Romanus was surprised when his name was called out repeatedly by the examiner. Once he realized he was one of the front runners, terror gripped him. He did not know if he would make a good pope. He certainly wasn't that good of an administrator. But the more votes he received, the more he became convinced that God could be calling upon him to perform more important work. He wasn't belittling the importance of managing the Holy See, but others could do that.

What he wanted to do with most of his time was to spread peace and good will throughout the world. Maybe it would be an idealistic and impossible goal to achieve, but if he was elected pope, he would certainly try.

CHAPTER 37

Max was genuinely worried about Frank. Not just worried, but frightened, too. With the "grand performance" drawing near, Max saw the toll it was taking on his brother-in-law. Frank had become obsessive and reclusive. He no longer bothered to gamble at the casinos. He took most of his meals in the privacy of his room chanting nonsensical phrases from the grimoire.

Originally, Max had been eager to read the grimoire, but now, he no longer wanted to have anything to do with a book that was destroying his best friend. Yes, his best friend. In the beginning, he knew Frank had tolerated him because he was Dottie's kid brother. How ironic things turned out to be. At the start of their unusual symbiotic relationship, Max had been in it for the money, and recently there had been a lot of it. But Max had grown to genuinely care for Frank. It hurt him to think that if Frank continued with the trances, the grimoire would destroy the only true friend he ever had.

Every time Frank came out of a trance, he looked older. His skin, now severely wrinkled, was the color of paraffin, pale, and sickly looking. It clung to his bony frame like dehydrated fruit. There were black circles beneath his eyes and the telltale age spots on his hands were that of an eighty-year-old man.

Before he began reading the grimoire, Frank had bragged about his hair because at his age, he didn't have any grey. Now the little he had was not only completely white, but it had lost all its luster and the few clumps he had left reminded Max of the hair he had once seen on a man in a cancer ward.

Although whatever was happening to Frank was giving him a Herculean mind, it was taking far more in return. The force inside him was like a parasite, a leach that had already sucked the soul out of one man, leaving a daughter fatherless, and now it was dangerously close of taking the life of his one and only friend. How he hated that book, detested it, wanted to destroy it, but he knew he never would. Frank was determined to have his day, and Max vowed he would stick by him to the very end, whatever that end might be.

* * *

It was two days before the performance. Frank had decided to call in sick so he could preserve, rest up, and conserve his strength. He had sent Max to watch the stand-in magician perform. It gave him a great sense of satisfaction when Max reported that the show turned out to be a flop.

Frank was still in bed the next day when Richard Stover pushed his way past Max and barged into Frank's suite at the Boulevardier. When Stover took one look at Frank, he backed up a few paces. "You really are sick, aren't you?"

Frank smiled wearily at Stover. "Don't you worry. I'll be doing a new show tomorrow. You had better come early as you might not get a seat."

"Very funny. I don't think that would be a good idea."

Although Stover's voice was barely audible, it cut into Frank like the blade of a serrated knife. "Like hell you say! I'm doing the show, like it or not."

"I won't allow it," Stover said. "You need to go to a hospital. I mean, look at you. You look like death warmed over."

The pent-up rage in Frank, his fury at Stover as well as the world, was about to spill over. He didn't want to unleash the full strength of his power on Stover because if he did, he might not be able to perform tomorrow. So he did the next best thing. He decided to scare the hell out of him. He kept an unloaded gun in his nightstand. Good thing, too, or he probably would have shot him. Very calmly and deliberately, Frank closed his eyes. When he opened them, the only thing Stover and Max could see were the whites of his eyeballs.

"No. Don't do it, Frank. He's not worth it," Max shouted.

"I'm sorry, Max, but I disagree. The pugnacious bastard has to be taught a lesson." Frank's lids flickered and the drawer to the nightstand slid open. The noise made both, Stover and Max, turn toward the direction of the sound. It only took Frank's mind a couple of seconds to remove the gun.

Stover's eyes widened as he first saw a steel barrel, then the trigger mechanism and a grip come out of the drawer on its own accord. The handgun made a pass over Stover and then hung suspended in midair not more than three feet from the man's nose.

The entertainment director stood motionless. Only his eyes moved. First to the gun, then to Frank, and then back to the gun again. The veins in Stover's neck ballooned when he saw the revolver's hammer and cylinder move. He barely got the words out. "Please, Frank . . . don't."

"What did you say about my not being able to perform?" Frank asked.

"Without removing his eyes from the gun, Stover said, "I can now see that you have been practicing."

The gun waved in midair. "You still haven't answered my question."

"If you are up to it, Frank. Only if you are up to it. Please . . . please put that away."

The gun dropped to the floor onto the carpet with a thud. "I think I should give you a slight preview of what you'll see tomorrow. Don't you think I should, Max?"

Before Max could respond, Stover, Italian loafers and all, raised up off the floor.

"Put me down, for Christ's sake," he yelled. "Put me down." No sooner had Stover uttered those words than Frank released his hold over him.

"Jesus," Stover said, in a quivering voice. "How did you learn to do that?"

Frank worked at keeping a straight face. "If I told you, then I would have to kill you."

"You're crazy," Stover spluttered. "You are both crazy!" He retreated to the door, but when he tried to open it, the door wouldn't budge.

"Before you leave, there is something you need to know." Frank said. "If you tell anyone what happened before tomorrow's show, you'll pay. Do you understand?"

All Stover could do was nod his head. The latch that had been holding the door shut clicked open, and Stover rushed out without saying a word.

Max was stunned. "Do you realize what you just did?"

"Oh, you mean pointing the gun at him? It wasn't loaded."

No, I'm not talking about the gun. What you did was . . . well, extraordinary."

"Come on, Max. It wasn't that big of a deal. You've seen me do more difficult things."

"You did what you did without the book!"

"I know. You can have the grimoire. I don't really need it anymore."

CHAPTER 38

Giuseppe had been locked in with the other cardinals for six days, and the conclave still hadn't elected a pope. After the examiners had burned fourteen ballots, he was now certain the election was between him and Romanus. It wasn't that he thought Romanus wouldn't make a good pope, but the problem with Romanus was that he was an idealist. Being a pragmatist, Giuseppe believed in getting things done while Romanus took the attitude that if he waited long enough, with God's help, the problem would solve itself.

Giuseppe was in the process of writing his name on yet another ballot, when he saw one of the Pontifical Swiss Guards approach the Dean of the Sacred College. The Guard whispered something in the Dean's ear and handed him a note. Then, much to his surprise, the Dean approached and handed him a folded piece of paper. "I have sad news. Your sister wanted you to know that her husband is in the hospital. The doctors told her he might not make it through the night."

When Guiseppe read the note, he crossed himself. "She says my brother-in-law is asking for me. He wants me to hear his confession and also perform the last rites."

"This is a bad time, I know," the Dean whispered. "It is your decision, but before you make it, you must know you can only leave if the conclave has no objection. If you decide to go, I will seek permission from the Cardinal Electors on your behalf. You can leave only if they allow you to leave. You must also know that if you decide to go, the voting will continue without you. You can return, but you cannot use a proxy to cast a vote in your absence. Needless to say, if you speak to anyone outside the conclave about any of these proceedings, you would be excommunicated from the Church."

"May I have a moment to think?" Giuseppe faced a conundrum. If he did not go to his brother-in-law's bedside, he would be remiss in his duties as a man of God and most likely would alienate his sister as well. And if he did go, there could be a chance that his absence from the proceedings would end up costing him the election. The Dean was waiting so he had only a few minutes to make his decision. He said a silent prayer. "Please God, help me make the right choice. Guide me to your wishes." He thought for another moment and then walked up to the Dean. "I must leave," he told him. "Would you mind speaking to the Cardinal Electors?"

The Dean nodded. He approached the examiners and asked them to cease counting the votes. Then, in a grave voice, he addressed the conclave. When no one objected, Guiseppe approached the two massive doors at which time the Swiss Pontifical Guards snapped to attention. The silence in the room was palpable, until it was broken by the sound of the doors being unlocked and then pushed open. The minute Giuseppe passed through the threshold of the Sistine Chapel, they were closed and relocked.

The sun was unusually bright, at least that's what Giuseppe thought, or maybe it was because he'd been cooped up in the Chapel for so long. He immediately notified his driver, and the two sped off to the hospital, a forty-minute drive from the Vatican. As soon Giuseppe arrived, he was rushed through the double doors of the emergency room and then ushered by a nurse to the intensive care unit. Carlotta, who had been crying, ran into Giuseppe's outstretched arms.

"What happened?" Giuseppe asked.

"He tried to commit suicide."

"How?" Giuseppe asked, stunned.

"A pistol," answered Carlotta between sobs. "I never even knew he had one. I didn't see him do it. I heard the shot, rushed into the bedroom, and there he was, lying on the floor. Oh, Giuseppe, there was so much blood. I talked to the doctors. They've done all they can, but it doesn't look good."

Giuseppe was taken aback. "But he is a Catholic. He of all people knows that's a sin."

Carlotta nodded. "You better go to him. He's been asking for you."

Antonio was on a steel gurney with two plastic tubes attached to his nose. His breathing was shallow and labored. Antonio rolled his eyes toward Carlotta and then toward the door. "I will be outside if you need me," she said.

It only took a few moments for Giuseppe to administer the last rites. He then bent over Antonio, took hold of one of his hands, and squeezed it ever so lightly.

"I am here, Antonio, and we are alone. You may confess your sins if you like." Giuseppe saw Antonio's lips move, but he had to place his ear next to his mouth in order to hear him.

"Forgive me, Giuseppe. For I tried to kill myself." Antonio was fingering his rosary. "I hope God in his reverence will understand." Giuseppe started to say something when Antonio pressed one of his fingers against Giuseppe's wrist. "There is something else. Oh, Lord God, I am so ashamed! I have done a terrible thing. I allowed Satan to enter my heart." Even with the oxygen, Antonio was having difficulty breathing. "The last time you were at the villa, I wasn't sick. I was angry. I wanted to hurt you, so I . . ." Antonio was now wheezing. "While you were having dinner with . . . Carlotta, I . . . opened . . . the safe. I took your briefcase and . . ."

Giuseppe struggled to hear the words. "Go on, Antonio. Go on."

"Wanted to get even . . . took papers . . . made copies . . . so sorry." After a few minutes, Giuseppe backed away. He knew Antonio would never utter another word.

With the movement of his right hand, Giuseppe formed a cross. Then in a loud clear voice, hoping Antonio could still hear, he said, "I absolve you of your sins." At that moment, Antonio took one more breath and his eyes glazed over.

Giuseppe stood for a moment, transfixed. He couldn't believe what he had just heard. Making copies of those notes was one thing, but what he wanted to know was what had Antonio done with them? He fought to get control of himself. His entire future, quite possibly becoming a pope, was now at the mercy of a dead man. Had Antonio planned to blackmail him? That had to be it! The last time Giuseppe talked to Antonio, the man had been frantic.

He had begged him for a loan. Giuseppe recalled Antonio telling him that unless he helped him, he'd be ruined, certainly the words of a desperate man.

Giuseppe knew people in distress were capable of performing despicable deeds. He'd heard confessions of murder, so why not blackmail? He had to think. What could Antonio have done with those notes? They were most likely at the villa somewhere, but where? Now he wished he would have lent his brother-in-law the money. A million and a half euros he had asked for. A small fortune, but the value of the trust was a hundred times that much.

Giuseppe used all of his willpower to gain control of his emotions. He told himself that he couldn't allow himself to panic. His sister needed him. He had to go to her. He left the intensive care ward and took his sister in his arms. "He is gone."

"Did you hear his confession?" Carlotta asked, weeping.

"Yes. Do not worry. He is with God now." Giuseppe wanted to leave. He wanted to return to the conclave, but he knew he would have to spend a few minutes giving comfort to Carlotta. She needed him now like she had never needed him before. He so desperately wanted to ask her if she knew about the notes, but if he did that, he would be violating a canonical law. For it was unforgivable for a man of God to breach the confidentiality of a confessional.

Giuseppe had to figure out a way to get those papers back before anyone else saw them. He had worried about a scandal, and now he found himself perhaps the catalyst of one. He had been a fool for taking those notes to the villa. But then who would have ever thought that Antonio, the very person who had worked so hard to have him elected pope, would have wanted to destroy him?

A chill coursed through Giuseppe. What if he was elected pope? Cardinal Callistus was aware he had those notes. If he was elected pope and a scandal ensued, what would happen? Would he be punished? Would he be absolved? Would he have to do penitence? Would his name be placed in some file in the Room of Dark Secrets?

Such a mess. And all because of a missing grimoire!

CHAPTER 39

Tonight was the defining moment in his life and Frank wanted to look his best for the performance. He had Max bring the Ferrari around so they he could pick up his new tux and cape from the tailor. He had lost so much weight that none of the half dozen tuxes hanging in his closet fit him anymore. Once he was satisfied the suit fit properly, he had Max drive him to a casino he had often frequented. "I want you to go to the casino's coffee shop. I'll see you there as soon as I can."

"Why are you picking today to play craps? We have so much to do to get ready for tonight."

Frank winked at Max. "We have plenty of time. I promise I won't be gone long."

A hundred thousand was Frank's goal. A fairly modest sum for a Vegas casino, particularly one on the Strip, but that would be a lot of money to Max. It was child's play for him to manipulate a pair of dice or a roulette wheel. Today it would be dice. He mouthed a few words, words he had committed to memory some time ago, and approached a crap table with a four-thousand-dollar limit. He took a wad of hundred dollar bills out of his pocket. No sooner had he placed the cash on the table, than a pit boss handed him his money back.

"What's wrong?" Frank asked.

"Aren't you Frank Santino?

"What of it?"

"I am sorry, sir, but I have strict orders not to allow you to gamble here anymore. No hard feelings, I hope."

Frank's face became flushed. "Oh, so it was okay for me to drop a couple of hundred thousand over the past four years, but it's not okay to try and win some of it back?"

"I am truly sorry, Mr. Santino. I just work here. I don't make the rules. If you would like, I can get the . . ."

"Forget it."

Max saw Frank heading toward him, his stride angry. "That sure was quick."

Frank's face was still flushed. "Shut up. Come on, let's go."

Max slipped behind the driver's seat. "Where to?"

"Take us to the Dixie Derby downtown."

When they were almost at the casino, Frank said, "Pull into valet parking. You are coming in with me."

"How come?"

Frank handed Max a fistful of hundred dollar bills. "The casinos on the Strip have wised up. They won't let me gamble there anymore."

"You know I'd do anything for you," Max said, "but I don't gamble. Hell, I don't even know how."

"You don't have to do a thing but keep placing money on the 'don't pass line.' I'll take care of the rest."

"How much should I bet?"

"Start out with a couple of hundred a bet. Then work your way up to five hundred. That's only when you don't have the dice. Once it's your turn to throw them, I want you to bet the maximum allowed. At the Dixie Derby, that will probably be two thousand a bet. Also, when you win eighty or ninety grand, I want you to ask the croupier if he will allow you to place a two-thousand-dollar bet on box cars."

"Box cars?"

"Two sixes. That's usually a sucker bet, but the payoff is huge." Frank laughed. "Today the suckers will be the guys who own the casino. They don't know this yet, but they are about to drop a bundle!"

Two hours later, Max and Frank walked out of the Dixie Derby each holding a bag. Once they were in the car, Max asked, "Why did you want to take the winnings in cash?"

"Just drive," Frank instructed. "You'll see." Frank told Max to head for the nearest bank.

"What are you going to do, rob it?" Max asked.

"This is no time for jokes. I want you to go inside and ask for a safe deposit box. The largest they have. Do you think you can carry both bags?"

"I guess so, but I still don't know what you're trying to accomplish."

"I'll tell you when you get back. And hurry, will you? We have to get to the amphitheater."

Twenty minutes later, Max jumped behind the wheel of the Ferrari.

"Do you have the key?" Frank asked.

"You mean the key to the safe deposit box? Yes, I have it."

Without any further conversation, Max started the car and turned north towards the Boulevardier Hotel. When they were almost at the amphitheater, Max asked, "What do you want me to do with the key?"

"Keep it. That money is yours."

"You didn't have to do this, you know," Max spluttered. "You have already left me well provided for. Didn't you say that if something was to happen to you, I'd get half of your estate?"

"Yes, but people have been known to do strange things when money is at stake."

"Dottie wouldn't try and screw me out of my share," Max said emphatically.

"You do know what the word 'insurance' means, don't you?" Frank asked.

"Of course I do."

"As long as you don't tell anybody, no one will ever be able to touch that money except you." Frank added, "I know you are really a smart guy, but sometimes I'm amazed at your ignorance. I doubt very much if Dottie would want to lay claim on the entire hundred and twenty grand, but she may insist you give her half. So I want you to keep your mouth shut. Don't tell Dottie anything about the money. I know she is your sister and that you love her dearly, but unlike you, she craves money like a junkie craves a fix. Now come on, step on it. We must get to the amphitheater!"

CHAPTER 40

Carlotta was inconsolable as she stood sobbing in Giuseppe's arms. He tried to comfort her as best he could. Finally, he said, "There is nothing more we can do here. Let me take you home."

On the way to Carlotta's villa, he tried to sort things out. What role did the notes play in Antonio's suicide? And how could he get them back? He turned to Carlotta.

"When you feel up to it, I have some questions I'd like to ask you about Antonio."

Carlotta fought back another snivel. "What would you like to know?"

"Do you have any idea why Antonio would do this?" He considered his next question carefully. "Did Antonio leave any kind of note?"

"Yes. All he said was that we were broke. And that you had been wrong about the Punta Dora project. He also said something that made no sense." Carlotta took a piece of paper out of her purse and read from it:

> My dear Carlotta,
>
> I am completely out of money. You know me. I could never live in poverty and would never allow you to support me. I am especially sorry I mortgaged the villa. I hope you will forgive me as I had no right to do that. But then again, I was desperate. I am also very sorry for what I did to Giuseppe. He was right to protect the money in your trust. I wish I could undo what I have done to him. It is such a shame that vultures are attracted to spoiled meat.
>
> Just remember, I love you.

Carlotta refolded the note and put it back in her purse. Tears were streaming down her cheeks. "I can't believe he would do this.

We could have worked something out." She turned to Giuseppe. "Do you know what he meant by that last sentence?"

Giuseppe mouthed the words, "It is such a shame that vultures are attracted to spoiled meat." He shook his head. "I don't have the faintest idea."

They rode in silence for a few miles. "You don't have to worry about the villa," he finally said. "I can pay off the mortgage from the trust."

Carlotta nestled her head against her brother's shoulder. "What would I do without you, Giuseppe? It's bad enough that Antonio is gone, but if something were to happen to you, I . . ."

"Nothing is going to happen to me. Nothing." Once they were in front of the villa, Giuseppe said, "I don't want to leave you, but I should get back to the conclave. Is there anyone I can call to stay with you?"

"Heavens no! You have to get back." She glanced at her watch. "My God, you've been gone for almost four hours. Don't worry about me, I'll be all right." She kissed him on both cheeks and turned to walk into the villa.

"Shall I take you back to the Vatican?" the driver asked.

Giuseppe was faced with another decision. His responsibility was to return to the conclave. He was given permission to leave only because a dying man had asked for him, and not to go chasing around Rome trying to solve a puzzle. He knew Antonio's reference to spoiled meat related to the notes he had copied from his briefcase, but what could vultures stand for?

"Is something the matter?" the driver asked.

"I don't know." Giuseppe replied honestly. "Take me back to the Sistine Chapel. And hurry!"

CHAPTER 41

Giuseppe was twenty minutes away from the Vatican. He needed to act fast. He pulled out his laptop, the one he always kept in the Chrysler, went online, and quickly found the telephone numbers he had been looking for. After closing the glass partition that separated him from the driver, he activated his cell phone. His hands were trembling so badly that it took him three tries to reach the right number.

"Let me speak to Mr. Aldobrandino, please." While he waited to be connected, he said a silent prayer for he now thought he knew who the "vultures" might be. He was glad Antonio had introduced him to one of the most influential men in all of Rome who just happened to own the *La Repubblica*, a daily newspaper with the largest circulation in Rome.

A booming voice came on the line. "Cardinal Mercati, I thought you were sequestered in the Sistine Chapel?"

"I shall explain later, Roberto. I need your help. It is important to the Church that you check with your editors as well as your reporters to see if any of them received an envelope or a package from an Antonio Draco."

"Are you talking about Carlotta's husband?"

"Yes. It could have come from him or possibly from an anonymous source. Please, it is imperative that your newspaper not publish a story one of your reporters might write from the information the envelope might contain."

"Can you tell me what this is about?"

"No. You just have to trust me, but as I said, it is very important to the Church." Giuseppe could hear the doubt in Aldobrandino's voice and prepared himself for the worst. He figured he'd soon find out if Roberto would place friendship and loyalty to the Church above a possible story.

Finally, he said, "I'll do what you ask. If I find the information, how do I get ahold of you?"

"Call me on my cell. You know the number. If the line is busy, please call back. I wouldn't ask this of you if it wasn't vital. No one, and I mean no one, should open the envelope containing those notes, including you."

"What if someone already opened it?"

"Reseal it and tell the person to disregard its contents. Will you do this for me?"

There was a pause at the other end of the line. "You are asking an awful lot, but yes, on the condition that you buy me the finest dinner in all of Rome."

"That's a promise," Giuseppe said. As soon as he disconnected, he punched in a series of new numbers. Giuseppe had one more person to speak to. Nazareo Remegio, a longtime friend, who was the editor-in-chief of *Il Tempo*, a daily newspaper with the second-largest circulation in Rome. As Giuseppe waited impatiently to be connected to Nazareo, he rolled down the Chrysler's window. He was close to the Vatican now, no more than five minutes away. That's when he saw the smoke. He said a small prayer to thank God it was black. It would take a while to poll the Cardinal Electors and tally the new votes. This meant he had just bought himself some time; how much, he did not know.

Guiseppe figured if Antonio was going to feed "spoiled meat" to the "vultures," he would have most likely picked one of those two newspapers. He had called *La Repubblica* first because it was the most popular newspaper in all of Rome. He doubted Antonio would have given *Il Tempo* the information because not only was it an extremely conservative newspaper, but it was pro-Vatican as well.

"Nazareo here." The voice was so distant Giuseppe figured it had to be a poor connection.

"This is Giuseppe. Can you hear me?"

"Yes, but what are you . . . ?"

"Please, don't ask questions. Just listen." After repeating his request to Nazareo, Giuseppe rolled down the glass partition. "Why are we stopped?"

The driver shrugged his shoulders. "There's been an accident, I think."

"Can you get me to the Sistine Chapel by using an alternate route?"

"Sorry, but I'm boxed in. All I can do is wait for the traffic to clear."

That's not what Giuseppe wanted to hear. Ten minutes passed. It was the slowest ten minutes of his life. Finally, the car was moving again. He was about to make a call to Carlotta when his cell phone buzzed. The sound startled him to the point that he dropped it on the floor. It took Giuseppe a few frustrating seconds to find it. "This is Cardinal Mercati." His voice was tense, guarded.

"It's Roberto. We did receive an envelope from an anonymous tipster. My editor was approached by one of our reporters who wanted to write a story about a four-hundred-year-old Vatican conspiracy."

Giuseppe's heart lurched. Maybe God had heard his prayer after all. "Do you have the notes?"

"Unfortunately, no. We told the reporter we could not publish an unsubstantiated story, so he left."

Giuseppe's hopes had been quickly crushed. "What do you mean, he left?"

"He quit and took the information with him."

Giuseppe was about to disconnect, when Roberto said, "There is only one place he could have gone and that's to a weekly paper here in Rome. It's called *Roma Sociali*."

"Why do you think that?"

"Because it's a filthy rag. The paper is owned by American News, although they would never admit it."

The news was worse than Giuseppe had thought. Americans always loved sensationalism. "Do you happen to know if American News owns any other papers? You know, newspapers that have a similar format to *Roma Sociali*?"

"Let me check." The line went silent for a few minutes and then Roberto was back. "One other. The counterpart to *Roma Sociali* is a paper called *Front Line News*. It's sold in the United States. Both papers thrive on sensationalism. They rarely bother to verify their sources. They often get sued, but they also sell a lot of papers. You won't believe how many people read that trash."

"Thanks, Roberto. I owe you." Giuessepe was faced with a choice. He could return to the conclave and quite possibly gain enough votes to become a pope. But by doing so, he would be risking a media scandal. Or he could attempt to retrieve his notes from *Roma Sociali* and save the Church's reputation and quite possibly his as well.

Whatever choice he made, he was sure of one thing. There wasn't enough time to do both.

CHAPTER 42

When Max entered Frank's dressing room, Frank was sitting in a chair with his feet propped up on the vanity table. A towel covered his eyes.

"What are you doing here?" Frank asked. "Don't you have preparations to make?"

"Sorry, but that's what I need to talk to you about. It's important."

Frank took his feet off the table. "All right, but make it quick."

"I've always done what you asked of me, but please, Frank, for your sake as well as mine, don't do this!"

Frank stood and placed his arm around Max's shoulder. "Do you remember my telling you the money in that safe deposit box for which you have the key is just an insurance policy?"

"I do, but this? I mean someone could really get hurt."

"And what do you think will happen if what I'm about to do doesn't work?" Frank began to apply makeup to his sallow face. "Look at it this way. If I manage to pull it off, no one will be the wiser. But if something goes wrong and you aren't there to back me up . . ."

"All right. You've made your point. I just wish to hell Dottie had never told you about my stint in the army."

An enigmatic grin appeared on Frank's face. "I'm glad she did. If I hadn't known you had once been a sniper, I would have probably come up with a different routine."

"It's still not too late," Max pleaded. "You can modify the act, make it safer. No one would be the wiser."

"You still don't get it, do you? I want them to remember me. I want to become the talk of the town. Just you wait and see. Houdini's stunts were mere child's play compared to what I'm about to do. I am going to make Stover and those other bastards eat their words."

Max knew Frank well enough to know when he had his mind set on something there was no changing it.

"Okay, I'll do it, but I sure hope nothing goes wrong."

"I hope so, too, because if you have to revert to our backup plan, I'll surely be a goner."

CHAPTER 43

A God-like figure stood framed in the middle of the black velvet curtains covering the stage. It was so still that most people in the audience thought the form had been painted on top of the fabric. That is, until the curtains parted. The audience gasped once they realized the shape was not a painting, but a man, and a very extraordinary one at that. Dressed in a gold-sequined tuxedo, he hovered four feet above the stage floor.

Like Christ, Frank Santino raised the palms of his hands outward to quiet the crowd. He had been jittery backstage, but now that he was in front of a live audience, he had no time to dwell on what might happen if his "magick" were to fail him. In order for the routine to work, he would have to concentrate as he had never had to concentrate before. It was imperative that he clear his mind of all thoughts; otherwise, he wouldn't be able to exert his remarkable power to the task at hand.

When Frank pointed to one of the side wings, a young female assistant approached, carrying a buggy whip. She waved it several times above Frank's head and beneath his feet to show the onlookers that he was not being supported by any invisible means.

Then Frank placed his fingers to his forehead and began to float even higher. He hovered six feet off the ground, the audience silent, their eyes glued to his body. While still suspended in midair, he positioned himself so his feet were now facing the ceiling and his hands were pointing toward the stage. Upside down, much like a rocket ship braking for a landing, he gently lowered himself, until his hands were two feet from the floor. Then, he righted himself, completed a somersault, and stood with his feet firmly planted on solid ground.

The audience jumped to their feet, giving Frank a resounding round of applause. For the first time in his career as an entertainer, Frank saw something he had never seen before in an audience. They looked at him with reverence, even awe, as if he were the Messiah.

A rush of adrenalin coursed through him. This was what he had hoped for. This is why he was placing his life on the line. No matter what happened it would be worth it, because tonight was his night.

* * *

Before Frank went into his final routine, Max climbed to the scaffold. It had been erected above the balcony so the technicians below could manipulate the robo-spots. Unfortunately, with all of the equipment it wasn't possible for him to lie in a prone position, so he crouched. Max was there because he loved Frank. He was the only person besides Frank who truly understood the grimoire's remarkable power, a power so strong that Frank had been willing to age prematurely in order to achieve his aims.

Max adjusted the scope of his Remington hunting rifle. He had confidence in the gun as he used to hunt with it all the time. When using a scope, he could hit a six-inch circle square in the middle from a distance of five hundred yards. The fact there was no wind to contend with and that his target was less than half that distance was a definite plus. But what worried Max was he would have to sever the spinal cord of his prey or else all hell would break loose!

He loaded the rifle with 7mm polycarbonate cartridges. The high-velocity bullets would literally explode on impact. The entry wound of the bullet would be no larger than the circumference of a dime, but a person would be able to place a bowling ball in the exit wound with room to spare. Max chose the bullets specifically for this occasion because they shattered on impact, and the last thing he wanted was to be responsible for collateral damage.

He felt the steel curve of the trigger, cool to the touch. Sitting there with his muscles cramped, Max forced himself to stay calm. Jittery nerves would often make a person jerk instead of squeeze a trigger, and if that were to happen, he could end up missing his target. Once he was in position, he tightened the rifle's sling. Max blew some air out of his mouth toward his forehead, changing the path of sweat rivulets that had formed on his forehead and had been heading toward his eyes. Now all he had to do was wait. In sniper land, waiting was the name of the game. There was a time when he would crouch, camouflaged, in full battle gear in some stinking hole for hours before picking off his quarry. For he knew an impatient sniper would soon be a dead sniper.

Max made a last a last-minute adjustment to the Leupold scope and sat there waiting, hoping against hope he would never have to squeeze the trigger.

CHAPTER 44

Before the deafening applause began to die down, Frank walked quickly behind a side curtain where there was a large mirror. After making sure his black wig was firmly in place, he reentered the stage to another round of deafening applause. Then, as he left for his dressing room, a group of tumblers and acrobats bounded onto the stage. He had hired them himself for the purpose of giving him a break—a chance to rest and mentally prepare himself for his grand finale, the *pièce dé resistance* of his career.

Frank thought of Max, hoping he was somewhere up in the rafters, patiently waiting in case Frank needed him to come to his rescue. It was rather ironic that only three months ago, Max had been a virtual stranger. Frank tried to think of how many times they had seen one another before he had asked for his help with the grimoire; a half dozen times perhaps. The more powerful Frank's mind had become, the more he needed Max close by. And now not only were they inseparable, but he was also entrusting his life to him.

Frank often asked himself the question: if he could live his life over again, would he do so with the grimoire? At times he thought maybe it would have been better for him to be broke than to be strong in mind but frail in body. He hadn't turned fifty yet, and already he looked like an eighty-year-old man. That was why he couldn't face Dottie. He couldn't live with the thought of having her taking care of his personal needs; the bathing, the shaving, the feeding. Not only would that have been humiliating, but he didn't think she would have the stomach for it. He just couldn't imagine her wanting to be seen with him.

So the end result would have been the same. He would have been relegated to a part of the house with no one but Max to minister to his needs. Hell, as of late, Max had to even assist him in using the toilet. No. It was better this way. She probably thought he was a bastard, but she'd get over it. Particularly once she found out he had left her the house and half of his money.

Frank wondered if she was out there in the audience watching the performance. He definitely was not the person he once was. And if Dottie was sitting anywhere near the stage, she would realize why he didn't want her to see him.

The wrap on the door jarred him back to the present. It was Pete, the stagehand. "Okay, Frank, better get ready. The tumblers and acrobats are about to finish their routine."

Frank quickly reapplied some makeup to his face. He decided that from a distance, even the most discerning person wouldn't be able to tell how he had aged.

Just as Frank made his entrance onto the stage, the lights dimmed and the orchestra began playing a haunting melody; one that some would later claim had a hypnotic effect, and what they had seen hadn't really happened.

All eyes were riveted on Frank as he picked up the microphone. The crowd sensed the magician who was standing before them was about to do something spectacular, something truly extraordinary.

Frank's mind was preoccupied with the task at hand. He was as ready as he would ever be. This was his moment, a moment he hoped to savor for quite some time. He had rehearsed the words he was about to speak so many times that, like a tape recorder, he could spew them out without thinking.

Frank had to hold the microphone close to his mouth; that's how weak his voice was. While his lips were forming words, his mind was replaying what would soon become a battle of wills.

"Most magicians perform tricks with the sleight of hand," Frank said. "They claim what they do is magic. A coin disappears from one hand and reappears in another. A handkerchief changes colors with the swish of a hand. All that proves is the magician performing such acts has dexterity, some would call it the sleight of hand. The levitation you saw me do earlier wasn't an illusion nor was it a trick. It was real 'magick.' "

As the music stopped, multi-colored spotlights flooded the stage. "I have prepared a very special final act for you. One you most likely will never see anyone else attempt. And one I hope you will remember for quite some time."

Frank paused long enough to peer out into the audience. Everyone who was anyone in the Las Vegas entertainment industry was there. Even Richard Stover, looking like he had just swallowed one of his cigars, focused all of his attention on Frank.

"The routine is quite dangerous," Frank continued. "But you needn't be afraid for I shall be in full control. I only ask that you stay calm and remain in your seats."

The silence in the room was so absolute that it added to the drama which was about to unfold. Every soul in the amphitheater clung to his seat and wondered what this amazing magician would do next. Expectations ran high and one could almost feel the tension in the air.

Just as patience among the spectators began to wear thin, the lights dimmed and a single spot focused its powerful beam on a strange-looking rectangular object. About the size of a small car, it was inching its way from the ceiling toward the center of the stage. Covered by a black canvas tarp, it was secured by a series of wires as thick as a man's thumb. The object slowed its descent and stopped once it was in line with Frank's head.

Two female assistants appeared, and in one swift motion, removed the tarpaulin to expose a steel cage. But it wasn't the cage that held the audience's attention. It was the panther inside. Its fur, smooth and silky, was the color of charcoal. The guttural growl that emanated from the creature caused the crowd some unrest, particularly among the onlookers sitting in the first row. Whenever the jungle cat snarled, it revealed a partially exposed set of fangs. Trapped, with hardly any room to pace, it searched for a way out of its steel prison. Whenever it moved, its clearly defined muscles would ripple, revealing to all not only its graceful agility, but also its strength.

Frank rolled his eyes skyward until his pupils disappeared from view. Once he was a foot or so from the cage, he placed his fingers against his temples. The locks that held the steel pins in place gave way. From an onlooker's perspective, the six sections that comprised the cage literally fell apart. They hung suspended for a second or two and then crashed to the floor. But no one was paying attention to the dismantled cage. All eyes were glued on the panther now standing in a fixed position in midair. It suddenly assumed a crouching stance as if it was about to pounce on Frank.

Like a virus let loose, a murmur spread from the audience. At that moment, two thousand people were convinced that the magician was done for. But to everyone's surprise, including the panther's, the cat was unable to strike. It could thrash its paws and swish its tail, but its movements were now more restricted than when it was in its cage. It appeared as if some invisible force was keeping the animal at bay.

The thunderous applause enraged the big cat even more as it clawed at thin air trying to free itself from Frank's vice-like grip. One of the female assistants handed Frank a whip. When he cracked it, the animal snarled. Frank cracked the whip again, but this time he did so above and beneath the creature. In doing so he removed any doubt the audience might have had about this being a trick. The animal was indeed transfixed in space.

Frank's two assistants walked from the wings, each carrying a large hoop made of brass. Frank took the hoops and ever so slowly began to circle the panther, and then, with lightning speed, threw one of the hoops towards the cat and then the other. Both found their mark as each hoop landed at the cat's midsection before sliding off the animal's back onto the floor. The panther went into a rage.

Alert as ever, Frank kept his eyes leveled on the snarling cat as it continued to make furtive attempts to claw his face.

It was just Frank and the panther. Their laser-like eyes were focused on one another. Frank instinctively knew the panther was trying to stare him down. The cat was doing it for no reason other than for its own survival.

It was man versus beast, two gladiators having a battle of wills, with the panther definitely having the physical advantage.

CHAPTER 45

Exactly four minutes into the act, a stagehand flipped a switch, and a second cage began its descent toward the panther. Frank's idea had been to imprison the cat before his will snapped and he lost control. He knew it would be a tricky maneuver because the cage had to come down slowly. If it were lowered too quickly, it would either miss its mark, or worse yet, hit the animal. Frank believed either occurrence would snap him out of his trancelike meditative state.

All it would take is for Frank's mind to falter, one slip, and it would all be over . . . unless, of course, Max did his part. Without taking his eyes off the panther, Frank envisioned the cat's head to be the target. Unless the bullet hit the cat in the kill zone, Frank most likely wouldn't live to see another day. Intuitively, as he tried to stare down the panther, other thoughts had already started to tug at his mind, a sure sign he couldn't hold his focus much longer, particularly on an enraged animal that wanted to kill him.

Three minutes had come and gone. An eternity when one's life depended upon keeping a creature that weighed close to two hundred pounds from clawing you to death. The closer the prison of steel was to the panther, the more the animal fought Frank's hold.

Just as the cage was about to imprison the cat, two thousand people gasped as the muscular creature hit the stage floor. Within a split second, the panther reared back on its haunches as it prepared to strike.

That was when Frank's mind entered a place of perversity where up was down, pleasure was pain, and madness was sanity. The instant that happened, the force that had allowed Frank to hold the panther in place, left him. He no longer had control.

Much as if someone had just released a coiled spring, and faster than a person could blink, the jungle cat leaped toward the people sitting in the front row.

* * *

From the moment Frank had freed the panther from its cage, Max had leveled the scope of his rifle on the animal. He had selected this particular gun not only for its accuracy, but also for the damage a hollow-point bullet would cause. He used the singular tense because he knew he would only have one try at it. The second Max realized the panther was free from Frank's hold, while the creature was still in midair, Max squeezed off a shot.

The audience screamed as the bullet imploded inside the lower portion of the animal's jaw. The high-velocity missile plowed through the rear of the panther's throat and vaporized its spinal cord into a thin, pink mist. Only a few metal shards had actually exited through the back of its throat, but it had left a gaping hole so large it had almost decapitated the animal.

Thinking this was all part of a well-rehearsed act, the audience went wild with approval. Frank listened with satisfaction as he struggled to take his bow before he slumped to the floor. As the stage curtain came down, Frank lay there unconscious.

"Let me through," Max yelled at the stagehands. "Call 911." He knelt by his friend's side, afraid for his life. As soon as the paramedics arrived, they checked Frank's vital signs.

"His blood pressure is very low, but he still has a pulse," one of the medics told Max. They placed Frank on a stretcher. One gave him oxygen while the other inserted an IV.

Max looked at Frank's frail body. He didn't think he weighed more than a hundred pounds. What was once a vibrant, healthy and relatively young man was now just skin and bones. He rode with him in the ambulance to the emergency ward where one of the nurses steered him toward a waiting room.

"Are you a relative?" she asked.

"Yes." Max was proud he didn't have to lie, proud to be considered family with Frank.

"I'll have one of the doctors come and talk to you once we know more about his condition."

"Can't I go in and see him?"

"Later, maybe. The doctors need to be alone with him right now."

Alone. If Frank died, for all practical purposes he'd be the one alone. Max knew there would be an inquiry and there would be a lot of people asking questions, questions for which he had few answers.

But that wasn't important right now. Max said a silent prayer. It was that damned grimoire. Whether Frank lived or died, he knew he had to get rid of that cursed book.

CHAPTER 46

As the driver sped toward the building that housed *Roma Sociali*, Giuseppe planned his strategy. He had to convince the editor not to print the story. But how could he do that? The answer was simple. He would offer him so much money that he would be hard pressed to refuse. After all, what did Giuseppe care? He would eventually donate his share of the trust to the Church anyway.

The driver veered around a corner and came to a stop in front of a red brick building with a large sign; the big, letters across its façade spelling out the name, *Roma Sociali*. Giuseppe was almost at the front door when he suddenly stopped, strode back to the car, and quickly got in. "Take me to the Vatican," he told the driver.

How could he have been so stupid? He would have made a terrible mistake had he walked through that door and asked for those notes. He could have just as well signed his name to them, as he would be admitting that everything he had written on paper was true.

What could he have been thinking of? Offering money for the information would have made a bad situation even worse. He could see the headlines now: CARDINAL OFFERS BRIBE NOT TO PUBLISH VATICAN CONSPIRACY.

As Prefect of the Secret Archives, he would be admitting to the entire world the duplicity of the Church.

His action would have most likely catapulted the scandal onto the world stage. Once there, it would have spread like the plague. Every newspaper and wire service in the world would be tripping over one another to pick up on the story. Even though the conspiracy was centuries old, people loved to read about scandalous misdeeds, particularly if the perpetrators were men of the cloth.

What was done was done, and no matter how hard he tried, he would never be able to change the course of events. The story would unfold in due time, he was certain of that.

Within half an hour, the walls of the Vatican were in sight.

For some inexplicable reason, the private gates intended for the clergy were closed so Giuseppe's driver had little choice other than to use the main entrance. Once inside the Vatican, Giuseppe told the driver to head toward the Ponte Sant'Angelo along the grand approach of the Via della Conciliazione, which was the main thoroughfare leading to the Basilica. The Vatican police were re-routing traffic, but when they spotted the Chrysler with its official seal of the Holy See, they let the car pass. As it moved at a snail's pace toward Saint Peter's Square, Giuseppe said a silent prayer. Maybe if he was lucky, he could reach the conclave before a pope had been chosen.

As if drawn by a magnet, people by the hundreds passed the Chrysler, and all of them were heading towards the Basilica. Fifteen minutes later, he saw it: the dome of the Basilica and the colossal Tuscan colonnades that framed the trapezoidal entrance to the majestic cathedral. Giuseppe thought of the colonnades as the arms of "Mother Church," always ready to embrace those who passed through its marble halls.

Once the Chrysler was several hundred yards away from the colonnades, the crowds had completely choked off the boulevard. That's when Guiseppe decided he could get where he needed to go faster by walking. After telling the driver he would no longer require the car, Giuseppe melted into the crowd.

* * *

Cardinal Romanus sat quietly in the conclave as the ballots were counted. For a while it seemed as if the votes were see-sawing: one for him, two for Giuseppe Mercati, two for him, and so on. Then he heard his name being repeated over and over: "Romanus, Romanus, Romanus, Romanus, . . ." Two tallies later, the two-thirds plus one vote had been reached. He was so overwhelmed that tears welled in his eyes. He had never expected this to happen, never campaigned, never thought he had a chance to win, but here he was about to be named pope.

As was the custom, immediately following a papal election, the Cardinal Dean, acting in the name of the entire electoral college, approached him. In a clear voice for all to hear, he asked, "Do you accept your canonical election as Supreme Pontiff?"

Romanus knew he was free to say, "non accepto." In the history of the Catholic Church, only one pope had ever done so because it was assumed that a candidate who was in contention to win the election would have informed the Cardinal Dean during the balloting process if he had no desire of becoming a pope.

If Romanus accepted, the Church would be placing an enormous responsibility on his shoulders, a responsibility he was not eager to assume, but because he was certain this was God's will, he took a deep breath, let it out, and said, "I do."

"What name do you wish to bear?" the Cardinal Dean asked.

"I shall keep my birth-given name," came the reply.

The Cardinal Dean bowed, turned toward the other Cardinal Electors and announced, "Be it known to the Master of Pontifical Ceremonies and the Cardinal Electors that the Bishop of Rome is to be called Pope Romanus the First."

It would only be after Romanus was ordained that he would be declared a true Bishop of Rome, true Pope, and head of the Episcopal College. Once that occurred, he would be in a position to exercise the full and supreme power of the universal Catholic Church.

Next, Romanus entered the "Room of Tears," a small red room adjacent to the Sistine Chapel. No one really knew why the room had been given such an unusual name; however, most clergymen believed that a pope-elect needed a place of solitude where he could contemplate the enormity of his newly-acquired responsibilities; the reasoning behind the room's name emanated from the co-mixture of grief and joy a newly elected pontiff most likely felt.

It was in this room that Romanus dressed himself. He chose a set of pontifical choir robes that included a white cassock and a red elbow-length cape with a hood. After he placed a gold pectoral cross around his neck, he reentered the Sistine Chapel.

Once formalities had been observed in accordance with the Order of the Sacred Rites for a conclave, one by one the Cardinal Electors came forward to offer homage and obedience to Pope Romanus. At that time the Senior Cardinal Dean gave the Apostolic Blessing, "*Urbi et Orbi*"—to the City of Rome and to the World—which was the standard opening of Roman proclamations.

CHAPTER 47

Giuseppe squeezed his way through the throngs of people as he desperately tried to get closer to the main balcony of the Basilica's façade. His eyes lifted skyward toward the Sistine Chapel. So far so good. He couldn't see any smoke, black or white. Giuseppe was fast approaching the elliptical center of the piazza where the Egyptian obelisk stood in all its splendor. Supported by lions made of bronze, the four-sided monument shaped out of red granite seemed to reach toward the heavens. Giuseppe thought it was prophetic that the obelisk, which had presided over countless Christian executions during Nero's time, now stood in the very spot that epitomized the magnificence and the glory of the Roman Catholic Church. "So many splendors and scandals," Giuseppe murmured under his breath.

Although Saint Peter's Square was virtually a logjam, he somehow managed to squeeze his way through the throng of people to within a hundred yards of the main balcony of the Basilica's façade. That's when he heard the church bells ringing. In his mind that only meant one thing. When he glanced toward the Sistine Chapel, his suspicions were confirmed. White smoke! It rose from the chimney which protruded from the Sistine Chapel sending a clear message that the conclave had chosen a pope.

At any moment the Cardinal Dean would walk out onto the balcony and make the long-awaited announcement. And when he did, Giuseppe would either go down in the annals of history as Pope Clement the XV, for that is what he wanted to be called, or he would fade into obscurity among the thousands of other cardinals who for the past twenty centuries had also wanted to become popes.

The defining moment had finally arrived. When the Cardinal Dean stepped out on the balcony, Giuseppe fingered his rosary, then, in a mere whisper, said, "Oh, Lord God. Please let it be me."

With hands outstretched, the Cardinal Dean waited for the boisterous crowd to settle down. Giuseppe tried to move closer, but it just wasn't possible. He heard a loud squawk and then the amplified voice of the Cardinal Dean:

"I announce to you a great joy. We have a Pope! The Most Eminent and Most Reverend Lord, Lord Oservatore, Cardinal of the Holy Roman Church, Romanus, who takes to himself the name Oservatore Romanus the First."

Giuseppe felt like someone had knocked the wind out of him. He never thought Romanus would be able to obtain the necessary votes to become pope. It had been a mistake to leave the conclave, particularly since the man he had gone to see had betrayed him.

He began to speculate. Would the election have turned out any differently if he hadn't left the conclave? Would he have been able to sway a few more votes his way?

With a sad heart, Giuseppe made his way toward the Sistine Chapel. Although the voting was now over, he had to see the new pope. He had to tell him about those notes.

* * *

Pope Romanus was exhausted. He had been sequestered with the other Cardinal Electors for nine days. The entire balloting process had taken much longer than he had expected. He wasn't quite sure whether God or fate had intervened in his behalf, but he did know this. If Cardinal Mercati hadn't left the conclave, he would have assuredly been the new pope. But all that was history now and made no difference whatsoever. Cardinal Mercati would never know how close he came to becoming pope. The rules of the conclave were quite specific. If a Cardinal Elector left the conclave, he was not privy to the information discussed in his absence.

After Pope Romanus had given the congregation his blessing, and thanks had been given to God, most thought the pope would retire to his private chambers, but not this pope. He sat down in the pontifical chair to hear from those Cardinal Electors who had pressing matters to discuss with their new Pontiff.

Romanus had listened and had dispensed advice to the Substitute Secretary of State, the Prefect of the Pontifical Household and five other cardinals when he spotted Cardinal Mercati standing in line. When it was Mercati's turn to approach, Giuseppe came to his knees and kissed the hand of His Holiness. "I shall pray for you, Holy Father. I am ready to serve you in whatever capacity you wish."

Pope Romanus acknowledged Giuseppe with the nod of his head. "Is there a reason you decided to see me on this particular day?" The question was asked without malice.

"Yes, Your Holiness. I know you have many things on your mind, but I need to speak with you in private. It is a matter of urgency."

Romanus wondered what was so important that the former Prefect of the Secret Archives was requesting an audience.

"How much time do you need?"

"An hour at most."

Romanus glanced at his secretary. "Is the appointment book filled for tomorrow?"

"Yes, Your Eminence."

"What time is my last appointment?"

"Nine o'clock in the evening."

"Schedule Cardinal Mercati for ten o'clock." Pope Romanus peered at Mercati. "I shall expect you in my private chambers by quarter to ten." Romanus couldn't resist adding, "Please be on time."

CHAPTER 48

Giuseppe entered the pope's apartment at nine-thirty. As he waited to see the Holy Father, he thought about the awkwardness of the situation. Although his encounters with Romanus had been rather few and brief when he had been a cardinal, Giuseppe had always sensed the man disliked him. What he didn't know was why. Was it personal? Or was it because their ideologies were so different? Giuseppe hoped Romanus could be objective.

Needless to say, Giuseppe's behavior had been inexcusable, but what really bothered him was he had broken an oath, an oath he had sworn to uphold as Prefect of the Secret Archives. Now, because of a careless mistake, his career, his very life was in the pope's hands. He thought it odd that fate worked in such strange ways. If he had only taken the time to place his briefcase inside his living quarters before heading out to see Antonio and Carlotta. If he had left the notes in either the Secret Archives or the Room of Dark Secrets, he could have very well been the one sitting in the pontifical chair.

Giuseppe knew Romanus well enough to know he would introduce an agenda far different from the one he would have chosen had he been elected pope. Romanus would continue to cling to old ways. Not that there was anything wrong with maintaining tradition, but Giuseppe had wanted to become a pope because he firmly believed the Catholic Church needed to be restructured. If he had had his way, parishioners would be given more latitude to perform religious observances that more closely met their needs. The Church was steeped with so many archaic traditions Giuseppe wondered if Romanus would take into consideration that those who came to pray were now living in the twenty-first century.

For now, he had to forget about all of that. Earlier he had pledged his allegiance to Romanus, and above all else, Giuseppe would keep his word.

At precisely ten o'clock, he was led into a room that had become familiar to him during his short tenure as Prefect of the Secret Archives. As Giuseppe approached the new pope, Romanus pointed to a nearby chair. "We can dispense with formality. It has been a long day, and I am not accustomed to working such late hours."

If it had not been for the urgency of the situation, Giuseppe would have waited a few days before making an appointment. He told himself he would have to learn to swallow his pride, particularly around this man. "I have come to tell you that I have inadvertently placed the Church in an untenable position, Your Grace."

"Untenable to me means indefensible. Is that what you mean?"

Romanus hadn't wasted any time in placing him on the defensive. Giuseppe decided he would have to choose his words carefully.

"Indefensible most certainly describes my foolish act. If you would allow me, I would like to start at the very beginning."

"That's always a good place to start," Romanus said.

Giuseppe wasn't sure whether the statement was said in sarcasm or if this was just Romanus's way of conveying humor. He realized if he didn't stop trying to second-guess Romanus, he would most likely end up getting tongue-tied.

Giuseppe related all the events from the time Romanus had come to seek his help in finding *The Testament of Solomon* to the recent conversation he had had with the owner of *La Repubblica*. Although he was as concise as possible, the story still took a good fifteen minutes in the telling.

The pope listened attentively without saying a word. Giuseppe thought that was an admirable trait and wondered if he could have done the same.

When he finished, Romanus leaned into his chair. "I want to make certain I understand what you have just said. Because our departed pope had been gravely ill, you approached the Prefect of the Ecumenical Penitentiary with the idea of destroying certain documents, several memos as well as correspondence, that dealt with the grimoire in question. You went on to say that because it was forbidden to remove anything from the Secret Archives and from the Room of Dark Secrets, you took notes, notes you felt would enable you to explain what had taken place some four centuries ago. Is this not correct?"

"Yes, Holy Father."

"Because Cardinal Callistus had to postpone his meeting with you till the next day, instead of leaving the notes in the Room of Dark Secrets, you placed them in your briefcase and took them to your sister's house."

"I had her place the briefcase in her safe," Giuseppe had been quick to add.

"Yes. So you said, for which your brother-in-law had the combination. Isn't he the brother-in-law who asked you to hear his confession?"

"Yes. My sister, Carlotta, managed to get a note through to the Cardinal Dean. In the note she stated that my brother-in-law, Antonio, was dying and wanted me to give him the last rites."

"The suicide note is what led you to believe Antonio had taken the information to the newspapers?" Romanus asked.

"One in particular. But because the notes were unsigned, *La Repubblica* had refused to print the story. Although *La Repubblica* refused to publish the account, the reporter who had my notes sold the information to *Roma Sociali.*"

Romanus cringed. "I've been told that paper publishes trash. Is this true?"

"So I've been told. I also heard their stories are hardly ever substantiated. I plan on getting ahold of the latest copy so I can see for myself."

"At least you had the presence not to sign your name to those notes," the pope said.

Giuseppe shuddered at the thought of what would have happened had he walked into the offices of the *Roma Sociali.*

"Not only were the notes unsigned, Your Grace, but the paper had no idea where the information had come from."

"Thank God for that. Tell me, Cardinal Mercati, what made you think taking notes from sensitive information in the Room of Dark Secrets was any different from removing the actual files? You took an oath to maintain the secrets of the Church, or had you forgotten?"

Giuseppe lowered his head. For the first time in as long as he could remember, he was having trouble in articulating his feelings. Normally words flowed from his mouth with hardly any effort, but not today.

"I know, Holy Father. I didn't think. I was so concerned that if the information were to ever leak out, it would further damage the reputation of the Church."

The pope appeared to reflect on what Giuseppe had just said. "I see. So let me get this straight. You were so concerned a vile conspiracy that occurred more than four hundred years ago would damage the Church that you took it upon yourself to disclose it?"

Giuseppe's cheeks turned the color of a ripe tomato. "I made a mistake," was all he could think of to say.

"You are an opportunist. You wanted others within the Church to know you had found out about the horrific deeds that some cardinals and a few priests had committed centuries ago, and then you took it upon yourself to bring the matter up before a prefect who, in a pope's absence, could have given you permission to have the documents destroyed. What a shame. Because of your unconscionable behavior, the very thing you claimed you were trying to avoid has actually happened."

Giuseppe couldn't believe it. It was one thing to be chastised by the pope. He had it coming, but he didn't think Romanus would have resorted to ridicule to do so. Giuseppe's face was not only flushed from embarrassment, but he was also angry, angry for the verbal thrashing Romanus was giving him.

Giuseppe flapped his hands against the sides of his robe. "I came here to tell you I made a mistake. I am sorry. I wish I could undo the wrong, but I can't."

"I shall have to give some thought as to your punishment," the pope said gravely. "You violated a canonical law, but right now I am more concerned as to how we can control the damage your reckless behavior has caused. I want to meet with the prefect who is in charge of public affairs. He will know what position we should take regarding this matter. Now, if you don't mind, I would like to retire. I anticipated that my first full day as pope would be a trying one, but never would I have guessed it to be this stressful. I suggest you pray to God for enlightenment, as will I."

Giuseppe kissed the pope's ring and left. The spring in his step was no longer there. He was disgusted with himself, and if this matter became an international scandal, he knew he only had himself to blame.

CHAPTER 49

After he had met with Pope Romanus, Giuseppe left the Vatican. He instructed his driver to find a newsstand where he purchased the latest copy of *Roma Sociali*. The first thing he did was scan the paper to see if the four-hundred-fifty-year-old conspiracy had been published. When he couldn't find anything, he remembered the paper came out weekly. That meant at the earliest, the story wouldn't break for another five days.

Once back in his apartment, he read the paper from cover to cover. The current issue contained a story about a woman giving birth to a three-headed baby. Another article claimed that Hitler's body had been taken to Argentina and placed in a cryogenic laboratory where it was frozen in liquid nitrogen in the hope he could be resuscitated at some future point in time.

But it was the lead story that really caught his attention. It was about some magician in Las Vegas who was able to suspend a live panther in midair by using the power of levitation. The panther, according to *Roma Sociali*, had broken free from the magician's spell. However, before it could injure anyone, a bullet had shattered its skull. No one knew who had fired the shot. The paper also claimed that Richard Stover, the director of entertainment for the Boulevardier Hotel and Casino, had not authorized a magician by the name of Frank Santino to put on such a dangerous act.

Giuseppe folded the paper and placed it in his briefcase. Three-headed babies, Nazis frozen in liquid nitrogen, levitating panthers. He wondered how people could read such drivel.

Two days passed. Each day Giuseppe bought a copy of all the major daily newspapers. He didn't think any of them would publish an uncorroborated story, but one never knew. Not only did he feel utterly helpless, but he felt anxious as well. Giuseppe was at a standstill, and would be until the pope made a decision as to what he was going to do. It was strictly up to Romanus to make the next move.

Finally, after four days and three restless nights, Giuseppe received word that the pope would see him at eight o'clock the following morning. Giuseppe had absolutely no defense. The only thing he could do was show the pope a copy of *Roma Sociali* and hope he would agree that no rational person with half a mind would believe such tripe.

His career, his entire future, rested in Pope Romanus's hands. The Holy Father had already told him there must be some kind of punishment. Now the question at the forefront of his mind was how severe would it be?

* * *

Giuseppe sat with the pope. It was difficult for him to get a read on Romanus as his face was expressionless. He knew this pope was all business, and he was anxious to share with him what he had discovered about *Roma Sociali*, but he sat there with his hands in his lap and waited humbly for Pope Romanus to take the initiative.

"Have you prayed for enlightenment?" the pope asked.

"I most certainly have, Your Eminence. But apparently God in his wisdom wanted me to take some initiative."

"And what did you do?" Romanus asked.

"I have a copy of the *Roma Sociali*, the paper most likely to print the story." Giuseppe was reaching into his briefcase to pull it out when Romanus stopped him.

"That won't be necessary. I've already seen the paper, and its American counterpart, *Front Line News.* I've also met with Cardinal Perugino whom you probably know. What you most likely don't know is I have appointed him as Prefect in Charge of Public Affairs. Cardinal Perugino told me those two papers will almost certainly publish the story. And although the cover-up is over four hundred years old, he said they'd make it appear as if it had happened yesterday. Fortunately the story can't be substantiated, but it will still mar the reputation of the Archdiocese. I say this because of the latest round of accusations made about our Church. I'm referring to the scandalous conduct of certain cardinals and arch-bishops who had been harboring pedophile priests."

Pope Romanus took in a breath and exhaled. "However, Cardinal Perugino seems to think all of this will blow over, providing no official statement is made by anyone within the Vatican." Romanus's eyes bore into Giuseppe. "You will be approached by newspaper reporters, of that I am sure. These people are not fools. They will figure out that the files relating to the scandal are most likely stored in the Secret Archives. I say this because I sincerely doubt anyone outside the Vatican knows about the Room of Dark Secrets. They will also assume the leak came from you. The press knows when prefects resign upon a pope's death, they are almost always reinstated to their old positions by the new pope. Since you will no longer be Prefect of the Secret Archives, they'll add two and two together."

The pope's statement didn't surprise Giuseppe. Even if he had upheld his oath of office, this pope would have chosen someone else to take charge of the Secret Archives. What he wanted to know was whether Romanus planned to demote him. He could have him transferred to some parish outside of Italy, if he so wished. He was about to ask Romanus what lay in store for him, but then thought better of it.

"What would you have me tell the reporters, Holy Father?"

"Good question. I thought about that for quite some time. Cardinal Perugino has suggested you simply tell them you know nothing about the cover-up, but that would be perpetuating the same problems that exist in those ancient files. Wouldn't you agree?"

Another jab, Giuseppe thought. This one right in the gut.

"I think it would be best if you were not to comment at all," the pope continued.

"Your idea is a good one, and I shall certainly do as you ask."

The pope looked at Giuseppe sternly. "I have been praying to God for enlightenment, Cardinal Mercati."

"You mean about the mess I caused?"

"No. As I told you, the Church will survive. I thought long and hard as to what to do with you. In the beginning, I was ready to send you to Siberia."

"To Siberia, Your Eminence?"

"That was a joke. Sometimes a joke is good for the soul. You should remember that. Anyway, you did a stupid thing, but then we are all mortals, aren't we? At least you did what you did without malice. You also proved yourself to me."

"How so?" Giuseppe asked, surprised.

"Instead of staying in the conclave, which no one would have blamed you for doing, you jeopardized your chances of becoming a pope to hear the confession of a dying man. A man, who in his darkest hour, betrayed you."

"I did what I felt had to done, Holy Father."

"I know. Whether you realize it or not, you placed compassion ahead of your own ambitions. That speaks a lot for you. And that is what the Catholic Church is all about. People often wonder why we have a prefect who does little else besides show mercy to those of us who have strayed off the beaten path. Do you know the difference between civilized people and barbarians?" The pope answered his own question. "It's forgiveness. That's what the building blocks of Christianity have been founded on."

The pope looked at Giuseppe as a father looks at his son. "I cannot give you your old job back. And it's not even for the reason you might think. You see, you and I have different values. I believe whatever has happened in the past within the confines of these walls, good or bad, must be preserved. You, on the other hand, believe the vile ugly things, in other words the secrets of our Church, should be destroyed. I call that a conflict of interest."

"I understand, Your Eminence."

"Do you? I don't think you do. I believe in maintaining the traditions of the Church. And if one of its traditions is to keep the dirty laundry hidden in a drawer, then so be it. I, for one, do not believe soiled clothes should be destroyed. We all commit sins, Cardinal. Some are bigger than others. But then, let us not forget that even though we are men of God, we are still mortals."

"I think I understand now."

"Good. I would like you to take your old job back." For the first time Pope Romanus revealed a barely perceptible smile. "I must confess I probably made a mess of things for the short time I had it. I wondered how you ever managed to keep your sanity. The Vatican Library is much in need of a competent, computer-literate administrator such as yourself."

Giuseppe kneeled so he could kiss the Pontiff's ring. "I would consider it a privilege to serve you and the Church in that capacity."

"Good. Then there is only one more thing that must done, even if it is just a formality. You must do penance for violating your oath. I want you to see Cardinal Callistus. Although he is fully aware of what you have done, you still need to ask him to show you mercy."

Giuseppe thought it ironic that only a short while ago, he was the Prefect of the Secret Archives and now he would become a statistic. He was certain his name would eventually be added to a file that would most likely find its way into the Room of Dark Secrets. Giuseppe was at the door when the pope stopped him.

"I don't think I have to tell you that before Cardinal Callistus makes his decision, he will confer with me." For the second time, Romanus smiled, although this time his smile was broader. "I want you to know I am in your corner."

Giuseppe had to fight back tears. In the beginning, he hadn't been convinced that God had anything to do with the laborious and sometimes tedious proceedings of selecting a pontiff. Now he knew better. Giuseppe was certain he wouldn't have been as good a pope as Romanus. Maybe age brought wisdom after all.

CHAPTER 50

Frank left the hospital in a wheelchair. Max drove him home as he no longer had any use for the suite he had been renting at the Boulevardier. Dottie was still living at the house, but that no longer made any difference to him. She had insisted on seeing him when he was in the hospital. At first, Frank had resisted, but finally Max had managed to convince him that although Dottie loved his money, she loved him, too.

When Dottie first saw Frank, she started to cry. Max had tried to prepare his sister for the way Frank had changed, but it had still been a shock. Understandably so, for Frank had continued to age since his last performance at the amphitheater. Like a tree that had been deprived of water, Frank looked spent and withered. He mostly stayed in bed. Dottie made it a point to be gone most of the time, so Max took it upon himself to care for Frank. He would fix his meals, bathe him, and he would also read to him.

Some would have called it fate, others a coincidence that Max ended up reading the feature story of *Front Line News*. He read the entire article to Frank. When Max read the part about Archbishop Dominique throwing a priest into a fire over a grimoire, Frank sat up in bed. "Dominique was the archbishop who was given that letter of gratitude, the one I bought from the old bookseller." Frank took hold of Max's hand. "There was only one grimoire!"

"What do you mean, only one grimoire?"

"The bookseller told me there were two," Frank blurted out. "He said Hollingsworth had one copy and the Vatican had the other." Frank hadn't been so animated in quite some time. "Don't you see? The grimoire must have been stolen twice! The archbishop brought it back. We know that from the letter of gratitude I bought from the bookseller. The paper said the conspiracy had been uncovered while searching for a grimoire. That means someone else had stolen it. The Vatican turned down your application to read the grimoire not because they found the subject matter to be frivolous. It was because they never had the book in the first place!"

"Whether there were two grimoires or only one makes little difference," Max said. "But speaking of the grimoire, what would you like me to do with yours?"

Frank thought for a moment. "I want you to send it to the Vatican. It's their book, I'm sure of it. After all, how many grimoires would there be with a singed cover?"

"Shall I sign your name to it?" Max asked.

"No. I want you to sign yours. I gave you the book, or don't you remember?"

Max did as he was told. He sent the book in care of the Vatican Library. The note simply stated, "I believe this belongs to the church."

* * *

Four months passed before Max received a reply. In the interim Frank had died. Max had been in the room when it happened. He was devastated, but it wasn't as if he hadn't expected it. In retrospect, he thought Frank passed away because he had nothing more to live for, not after his spectacular performance.

Frank's death had left a void in his life. He had been like a brother to him. Max had never had such a close friend, a friend he knew he would never forget for as long as he lived.

The police hounded Max for some time. They suspected he had been the one who killed the panther, but Max had been smart. The day after he had shot the cat, he buried the rifle, and with no tangible proof and no witnesses, the only thing the police had was their suspicions.

Max was living with Dottie in Frank's old house when a letter arrived from the Vatican addressed to him. When he opened it, he was shocked that the pope himself had signed it. But what surprised him even more was the letter had been handwritten. He wished Frank could have been here as he knew he would have been proud of him. He was so excited that he read the letter to Dottie several times:

> Dear Mr. Hunter,
>
> You will probably recall that your application to read *The Testament of Solomon* was denied, but it was not rejected because your request had been a frivolous one.
>
> In fact, at the time I reviewed your application, I thought you had a rather interesting premise. The real reason, as I'm sure you know by now, is because the book could not be found. It had been stolen once and then returned. No one at the Vatican suspected that it had been stolen a second time. I apologize for having deceived you. That was wrong, and I hope you have it in your heart to forgive me.
>
> What really touched me is that you thought enough of the Church to return it, particularly since you must have valued it a great deal. I say this, because otherwise you would have never requested to read it in the first place.
>
> If you should ever decide to take a trip to Rome, I would consider it a privilege if you would come and see me. I would like nothing better than to be able to shake your hand.

Max folded the letter and placed it in a Bible that was on top of the coffee table. Dottie put her arms around her younger brother. "You wish Frank were here, don't you, Max?"

"Yes, I do. What about you? Do you miss him?"

She took a handkerchief and wiped a tear off Max's cheek. "I loved him, but not like you. Never like you."

Did you enjoy this book?
Visit ForemostPress.com to share
your comments or a review.

Breinigsville, PA USA
08 December 2010
250872BV00001B/51/P